PHANTOMS IN THE SNOW

PHANTOMS

KATHLEEN BENNER DUBLE

IN THE SNOW

SCHOLASTIC INC.
New York Toronto London Auckland
Sydney Mexico City New Delhi Hong Kong

ISBN 978-0-545-39495-6

12 11 10 9 8 7 6 5 4 3 2 1   11 12 13 14 15 16/0

Printed in the U.S.A.   40

First Scholastic paperback printing, September 2011

FOR MY VERY OWN SPECIAL HERO,
BOTH IN WORLD WAR II
AND ALWAYS IN MY HEART:
MY UNCLE, LEONARD PALMER.
AND IN GRATITUDE TO THE MEN
OF THE TENTH MOUNTAIN DIVISION,
WITH SPECIAL THANKS TO PETER BINZEN,
MOUNT RIGA'S PHANTOM.

CHAPTER ONE

Noah Garrett sat on the kitchen chair and listened to the rhythmic ticking of the hall clock echoing through the nearly empty rooms of his house and to the two lowered voices coming from behind the hastily shut door, the minister's gentle and quiet, his neighbor's shrill and determined.

Through the window, Noah could see the grass in the fields moving back and forth, the sight so familiar that his heart ached with each gust of wintry February wind. And in the distance, he could see the headstones, two of them, tall and forbidding in the midst of the rising grass. CELESTE GARRETT, LOVING WIFE, DEVOTED MOTHER, JANUARY 12, 1944, on one; MITCHELL GARRETT, LOVING HUSBAND, DEVOTED FATHER, JANUARY 17, 1944, on the other.

Noah sat rigid with worry on that kitchen chair and listened to those voices and the clock and the wind coming in through the cracks of his house. And he waited for his future to be decided.

CHAPTER TWO

The door to the train compartment was thrown open, and two boys in uniform, one short, the other tall, came tumbling in, laughing and poking each other.

After hours on the train riding alone, Noah was startled by their sudden appearance. The boys pulled up short, almost knocking into each other. The rhythm of the train made them sway as if they were deliberately rocking back and forth on their toes.

"Well, well," said one boy. "What have we here?"

"A new recruit, it looks like," the other boy said. "Say, kid, you coming to Denver to learn how to fly? Did you just join up to fight?"

Noah shook his head as the two boys flopped down on the seat across from him.

Fighting again, Noah thought, *always fighting and the war.* The war against Germany, Italy, and Japan had taken a firm hold on the country ever since the bombing of the American naval base at Pearl Harbor in Hawaii. Everyone had rushed off to sign up and fight. Now, two years later, the battle seemed to have stalled. In Russia, the city of Leningrad was under siege, and America was losing more boys in the Pacific every day. Still, in spite of the bad news, Americans continued to sign up in droves to go and fight.

The taller of the two boys reached into his jacket and pulled out a flask. He took a swig and handed it to his buddy, wiping his mouth with the back of his hand.

"Where you headed, then?" the short one asked, taking a drink.

"Camp Hale," Noah answered.

The two boys grinned at each other and burst into laughter.

"Now, why would you go and join a military *skiing* division?" the tall one asked. "You should have been smarter. You should have joined up with the Air Corps like us, been a pilot. It's going to be us pilots, you know, who are going to whip those Germans and Japanese and win this war. That skiing division of yours won't be of any use at all."

"It's not *my* skiing division," Noah said. "I didn't join. I'm only fifteen. I'm being sent there."

"Sent to Camp Hale?" the tall one hooted. "Who would send a kid to Camp Hale?"

A minister and a neighbor, Noah thought, *that's who'd send a kid to Camp Hale; a minister and a neighbor who didn't know what else to do with him.* His parents were gone. His grandparents were dead, too. They said there was no other choice.

He thought of his mother and father — both pacifists. He remembered their talks with him about the war, how killing at any price was wrong. He imagined his mother's horrified face if she knew he was being sent to a military camp. He imagined his father's anguish.

He looked at the two boys across from him. Were they scared knowing that soon they would be sent to fight far from home? Had they even thought about dying or, like a lot of other boys who had signed up, did they see it all as one big adventure? Noah would never have signed up. Like his parents, Noah believed that war was not the answer to anything.

"You're awful big for fifteen," the short one said.

The soldier's statement was nothing new. Everybody said the same thing to him. His father had been proud of Noah's height. "We raise 'em big here in Texas," his father had said, laughing. His father had always had a loud, booming laugh, one that had embarrassed Noah sometimes. Now Noah would have given anything to hear that laugh again.

"You staying for a while at Camp Hale?" the short one continued.

"Depends, I guess," Noah said, looking out the train's window.

"On what?" the tall one asked.

"On what my uncle and I decide once I get there," Noah answered.

"Your uncle's a Phantom?" the short one asked.

"Huh?" Noah said, turning from the window to face them, caught by the sudden strange word.

"Phantoms," the tall one said. "That's what we call them, the soldiers that ski. You can't even see them when they're in the mountains. They disappear like ghosts. They can ski and hike faster than normal people. It's spooky."

"Not that that will help us win the war." The short one laughed. "I mean, we're fighting those Germans in the sands of Africa for God's sake. What are they going to do? Ski across the desert?"

"So," the tall one persisted, "is your uncle a Phantom or not?"

Noah gazed at the older boys across from him, their uniforms starched and pressed perfectly, their shoes gleaming with polish. He thought of his uncle, the man he had never heard of until his parents died, the man he had never met. Noah felt a wave of loneliness wash over him.

"Yeah," Noah said slowly, "I guess he is a Phantom."

CHAPTER THREE

The two soldiers finally slumped off to sleep. Noah fidgeted on the uncomfortable wooden seat of the train and stared out the window, watching the landscape turn from flat and brown to rocky, high, and white. He thought about what lay ahead of him.

Would he ever get over losing his parents? Or would he feel this sense of loneliness forever? His whole life had been his mother, his father, and the farm.

Friends? There had only been a few, and none particularly close to Noah's family, living as they had twenty miles outside of Austin. His mother had taught him his schooling at home. The only time he had even seen other kids was on their weekly visit to town for church or their monthly trip for supplies. Noah was used to being alone. But he was not used to feeling lonely.

And the future that now lay before him only increased his sense of loss. Who was this man he was being sent to?

What would he be like? Why hadn't his parents ever mentioned him?

And then there was the war issue. Even when his father had first taken him hunting, Noah had balked at shooting anything. "My gentle giant," Mama had called him when he had returned that first day with nothing to show after having been gone for hours. Noah had liked hearing himself described that way. And though he had eventually learned to hunt with his father, he never relished the trips.

He looked at the boys asleep across the aisle from him. Wouldn't German or Japanese boys look like that if he were sitting next to them? Wouldn't their heads droop the same way as they slept? Wouldn't their snores be soft and even, too? Noah could no more imagine shooting the boys across from him than he could imagine that they would shoot him back. How could they? Why would they? Why would anyone want to? It just didn't make sense.

Looking out the window of the train at that vast expanse of white, he felt his feelings mirrored in the countryside that flew by him. It was cold and bleak.

Three hours later, the train pulled into the station at Denver. The two soldiers rose groggily from their seats, their caps askew on their heads, their pants slightly wrinkled.

"Good luck, kid," the tall one said. "You're going to need it with that bunch at Camp Hale."

"Aw, don't scare him like that," the short one said, punching the tall one lightly on the arm. "He'll be okay."

He turned back to Noah. "Besides, I doubt they'll let a fifteen-year-old stay. You're too young yet to be on an army base. So don't worry about it. In no time at all, you'll probably be back home. Then when you turn sixteen, you can join up with a division that's really going to do something. You can join us pilots!"

The short one smiled, and the tall one saluted as he straightened his cap. Noah watched the boys leave the compartment, and the train was off again.

The soldier's statement surprised Noah. He hadn't considered the fact that they may not let him stay at Camp Hale. But he couldn't go back home. There was nothing there for him. Their house was for sale, the proceeds intended to pay off their farming debts. He would have to find a way to make the army let him stay, or he would have to come up with a plan to live by himself, a way to make it on his own.

Stay at Camp Hale or live alone. One or the other — those were the alternatives. An orphanage was not an option. This decided, Noah leaned his head back against the seat and fell asleep.

"Last stop! Camp Hale!" The conductor's voice rang out as he made his way through the train, banging on each of the compartment doors.

Noah rose slowly to his feet, stretching out his muscles after the train ride from Denver. He pulled his duffel bag down from the shelf above him and threw it over his shoulder. He walked down the corridor to the door of the train.

"Off you go, then," the conductor said, swinging the door open for him.

A rush of cold air and a foot of snow greeted Noah. He took three steps down, pulling his lightweight jacket tight around him.

Sprawled in front of him were hundreds of identical buildings. Row upon row stretched as far as he could see, whitewashed and dreary looking, a smoky fog curling just above the rooftops. And beyond the barracks rose the mountains, jagged and unyielding and yet strangely majestic. Noah had never seen so much snow or mountains like these, nor had he ever felt such cold.

A high, shrill whistle sounded, and the train began to pull away. Noah stood and watched it gather speed. A gust of wind blew through the train station.

The train rounded a bend, growing smaller and smaller. Noah suddenly felt horribly homesick.

He turned back to the barracks and the white mountains behind them. Snow swirled like dandelion fluff around him. No one was in sight.

He heard a creaking noise and turned to look. A wooden sign swung back and forth in the wind. WELCOME TO CAMP HELL, it said.

CHAPTER FOUR

Noah waited for his uncle. The snow picked up, until it was a wall of white, the flakes melting into dark spots on Noah's pants and coat.

No one came, and the cold and wet soon penetrated Noah's flimsy coat. He decided to walk into the camp by himself. He took several steps forward and then suddenly felt sick to his stomach. His head began to ache, and it was all he could do not to fall to his knees.

In front of him, in the middle of the swirling snow, a shape began to take form. It was white from head to toe, no face, no eyes, nothing. *A ghost*, Noah thought, too ill to feel fear.

Light-headedness swept over him, and Noah sank to the ground. The last thing he felt was the snow against his cheek.

| ▌ | ▌ |

He woke to the sound of laughter and the smell of coffee. He tried to sit up, but his head was pounding fiercely. He fell back against the bed he was lying on and moaned slightly.

Someone came and hovered above him. Noah focused on a man, a man who was deeply tanned and very tall with large bony hands and eyes with heavy wrinkles around them. His uncle?

"You okay, son?" he asked.

Noah tried to nod, then stopped. "My head hurts."

The man smiled. "Yeah, it happens to a lot of new ones here. It's the altitude, gives them headaches, makes them faint or dizzy. Don't worry. You'll get used to it."

Noah wasn't so sure. He couldn't imagine anyone getting used to a drum being played in his head.

The man drew up a chair. "My name's Harold Skeetman. Around here, they call me Skeeter. Can you tell me what you're doing here? We weren't due any new recruits for a while."

"My name's Noah Garrett," Noah said, holding on to his head. It even hurt to talk. "Do you know my uncle? James Shelley?"

A cautious look crossed Skeeter's face. "Yeah, I know him. Is he expecting you?"

Noah nodded. "I think so. My minister was supposed to write him that I was coming."

Skeeter looked Noah up and down, his eyes carefully assessing him. "How old are you, Noah?"

Noah paused. He remembered the soldiers on the train and the fact that at least for the time being, until he could figure out a way to live alone, he had to find a way of staying here.

"I'm sixteen," Noah answered. He was surprised at how easily the lie tripped off his tongue. He hoped his parents, if they were watching him now, would forgive him this small untruth. He would be sixteen soon enough.

"You visiting?" Skeeter asked.

"No," Noah said and then paused. "My parents died so I was sent here. I've never met my uncle before."

"Ah," Skeeter breathed.

Noah looked quickly at Skeeter, but there was no pity there, just sadness and an odd look of understanding.

"My parents are dead, too," Skeeter explained.

Noah nodded.

"Well," Skeeter said finally, "why don't you try and sit up? I'll take you to your uncle, and we'll straighten this all out."

Skeeter helped Noah to his feet. Noah's head pounded even harder. He felt like a complete weakling. Even his legs were shaking.

Skeeter handed him a wool coat, thick and warm. "You'll need this. That jacket you brought won't do you much good until early summer."

Noah slipped the coat over his arm, picked up his duffel bag, and followed Skeeter into a room filled with tables. Boys, a little older than he was, sat in the room, laughing and drinking coffee. Their cheeks were bright with color and heavy with stubble.

On the walls were life-size pictures of Hitler and Hirohito, their faces marked by pinpricks from darts that had been thrown their way.

As they walked by one of the tables, Noah heard someone say, "Yeah, the wind was so strong on that island that at night we tied our tent ropes to the wheels of our jeeps just to keep them down."

Other boys, listening, nodded.

"So anyway," the boy continued, waving his hands about as if he were a king holding court, "one morning, some soldier from another division gets up and forgets about those tents. And he gets in his jeep and drives off, pulling Wiley here" — he pointed to another boy sitting next to him with pale skin and a shock of red hair — "and his tent to the ground. So there was Wiley wiggling around inside like a worm and being dragged across the camp."

The boys at the table burst out laughing. Noah couldn't help it. In spite of his aching head, he laughed, too.

"Oh, you think that's a good story," the boy with the red hair retorted, putting his arm around the one who had told the tale. "Let me tell you one on Roger here."

Skeeter pulled open a door and motioned Noah out. They stepped into the cold. The camp was strangely silent, blanketed with the newly fallen snow. Skeeter didn't even pause but took off at a fast pace. Noah hurried to keep up with him, throwing on the heavy wool coat as he stumbled along. His feet sunk into the light powdery snow, and the thin air made the going difficult.

"Mr. Skeetman," Noah called out, breathing heavily, "at the train station, when I was standing there, I thought I saw something, something all white." He wasn't about to add "something that looked like a ghost."

Skeeter's chuckle drifted back to Noah on the crisp air. "It's Skeeter, son, just Skeeter, and that something was me. Our uniforms are all white. It keeps us invisible in the snow so we can escape or attack our enemy unseen."

Noah thought about the pilots he had met on the train and their derogatory comments about the worthlessness of these skiing soldiers. He wondered if these boys had heard some of that kind of talk. Noah knew he would hate for people to think of him as completely useless. Did it bother these soldiers?

Skeeter opened another door, to a much smaller barracks than the one they had come from. Noah followed him across the threshold.

The first thing that hit Noah was the smell, an awful burnt rubber smell. And then the girlie pictures, thousands of them pinned up all around the walls of the barracks — girls in bathing suits, girls in bras and underwear, girls with almost nothing on.

"Real men don't treat their women like that, looking at them half-naked. And women who pose like that, well, decent men don't consort with the likes of them," his father had once said.

Noah flushed.

Skeeter didn't give the pictures a glance. Instead, he quickly walked between the rows of bunks, and Noah found himself hurrying after him again. Finally, Skeeter stopped in front of one of the beds.

On a bare mattress with two crumpled blankets and no sheet, a radio clutched tight against him and liquor bottles on the floor all around, lay a huge bear of a man, snoring loudly enough to wake anyone within fifty miles.

Noah looked over at Skeeter.

Skeeter smiled apologetically.

"My uncle?" Noah asked, dropping his bag.

Skeeter nodded.

CHAPTER FIVE

Skeeter bent over the man and began to shake him awake.

Noah's uncle moaned and turned over, swinging an arm out at Skeeter, like someone trying to get rid of a buzzing mosquito.

Skeeter backed off until James Shelley lay still again. Then Skeeter went around to the other side and shook him, hard this time.

"What? What?" roared Noah's uncle, his eyes flying open. "What is it? Can't a man get any sleep in this place?"

Skeeter gave a slight laugh. "You got company, Shelley."

"Yeah?" Noah's uncle said, raising himself up on one elbow to peer at Skeeter. "Well, if it's that blonde from town, Skeeter, you get rid of her, okay? I ain't in any mood or condition for a woman's company right now."

"It's not a woman, Shelley," Skeeter said, nodding toward Noah.

"Yeah, well, then what?" asked the big man, swinging himself onto his other side and coming face-to-face with Noah.

James Shelley stared at Noah, and Noah stared back in shock. His uncle's eyes were glassy in his heavily bearded face, and his breath was terrible. But still, his uncle looked just like his mother.

"So, who's this?" James Shelley asked. "Is this a joke of some sort? Is that fool Pete trying another of his tricks?"

"No, Shelley," Skeeter said. "I guess this is your nephew, Noah Garrett."

"What?" James Shelley asked.

"I'm Celeste Garrett's son," Noah said.

"So?"

Noah's stomach lurched uncomfortably. These were hardly the first words Noah had expected to hear from his uncle.

"Your sister," Noah said, hoping that his uncle had just misunderstood. "I'm her son. She's dead, sir, and I've been sent to you because I don't have any other living relatives."

His uncle frowned. Noah waited. Would his uncle not tear up a little? Maybe welcome him here? Shake his hand? But the man said nothing.

Noah closed his eyes and took a deep breath, reminding himself that while sending him here had obviously been a mistake, his minister, Reverend Patterson, and his neighbor, Mrs. Norman, couldn't have known. This wasn't anyone's fault.

"Look," Noah managed to say in a patient voice, "I guess this isn't what you were expecting. It wasn't what I wanted, either. If you just give me a place to sleep for tonight, maybe we can figure out something else tomorrow, sir."

Suddenly, James Shelley's hand shot out, gripping Noah's arm tightly. His uncle pulled Noah closer, looking him up and down, still not saying a word.

Noah couldn't believe he was being treated so shabbily, especially by someone who looked so uncannily like his mother. "Forget the place to sleep!" he managed to choke out in a tight voice. "I'll just leave now."

"Whoa, whoa," Skeeter interrupted, holding up his hand at Noah's words. "Wait a minute, son. I'm sure your uncle is happy you're here. He's just surprised is all. Right, Shelley?"

James Shelley glared up at Skeeter. Skeeter glared back.

Noah waited. What was he supposed to do? Would he have to sleep out in the cold at the train station? Noah suddenly felt exhausted and overwhelmed and embarrassingly near tears. Determinedly, he gritted his teeth. He *refused* to break down in front of this unfeeling man.

Then James Shelley sighed. "All right, boy. I'll do something with you. We'll work this thing out."

"Good," Skeeter said, smiling. "I'll leave you two to get acquainted."

Skeeter walked toward the door and then turned to face Noah. "You come see me if you need anything, okay?"

Noah paused. Should he stay? What choice did he really have? There was no other place to go, at least until morning. Reluctantly, he nodded his agreement.

Skeeter opened the door and then was lost in a blast of cold air.

James Shelley swung his legs out from the blankets and stood up. "So, you say my sister's passed on, huh? You got a father?"

"He went, too," Noah said.

"Ah," James Shelley said. "You got any brothers or sisters I should know about? I mean, ten or twelve kids aren't going to suddenly descend on me or anything, are they?"

Noah shook his head. How could this man act so callous about his own sister's death?

"You hungry?" James Shelley asked.

The question threw Noah off guard. He nodded.

"Well, let's head on over to the mess hall, then," his uncle said. "I know I could use some grub."

Noah followed his uncle to the door of the barracks, where Shelley grabbed a jacket. His uncle went to open the door and then stopped.

"How'd she go?" he asked, not looking at Noah.

"What?" Noah asked.

"My sister," his uncle repeated impatiently. "What took her?"

"Smallpox," Noah answered.

James Shelley stood for a minute, his hand resting on the doorknob. Then without another word, he whipped the door open, sending it smashing into the wall.

"Let's go, boy," he said.

CHAPTER SIX

They headed back to the mess hall. When his uncle opened the door and stepped into the room, everyone looked up and started cheering.

James Shelley threw open his ski jacket and swept off his wool hat. He stood with his feet planted apart, grinning from ear to ear.

"Toast! Toast!" the boy, Roger, yelled, grabbing a bottle of whiskey and handing it to Shelley.

Noah's uncle lifted the bottle high. "To the mountains!"

The boys suddenly fell silent as they raised their own glasses. "To the mountains!" They each took a drink.

Noah watched his uncle put the bottle to his lips and drink half of it down. Everyone cheered again. Noah wondered what they were celebrating, but nobody seemed to want to enlighten him.

James Shelley turned and handed the whiskey to Noah. "Here, kid."

Noah stared at the liquor his uncle had given him. He was only fifteen, had never had a drink before in his life, and didn't want one now. He gazed at the bottle, wondering what he should do with it.

Skeeter came forward and took the whiskey away. "I don't think that's such a good idea, Shelley."

But James Shelley wasn't paying attention. The boy, Roger, had begun chanting, "Tell it! Tell it! Tell it! Tell it!" and the other boys stood and joined in.

James Shelley grabbed a chair and swung it around. He sat down backward on the seat, Roger and Wiley and the others all gathering close around him.

Skeeter touched Noah on the shoulder and motioned him toward the back. "Let's get you some food, kid."

Reluctantly, Noah followed him. As he moved farther away, toward the kitchen, he tried to hear what his uncle was saying, but the words were soon indistinguishable.

In the back, Skeeter handed Noah a tray and some utensils. He began dishing food from the cafeteria-style buffet onto Noah's plate.

The food made a loud plopping sound as it landed on the dish. Noah stared at the big brown glob. He wasn't sure if he was being served stew or slop.

Skeeter caught his look. "Not too appetizing to look at, eh?" He grinned. "And unfortunately, it's even less appetizing to eat!"

Noah laughed.

Skeeter handed Noah a glass of milk. "So, do you mind my asking? How'd your parents die?"

"Smallpox," Noah said. "Within a week of each other."

"Couldn't live without each other, huh?" Skeeter asked.

"Wish they'd realized that *I* couldn't live without one of them, either," Noah said.

Skeeter nodded. "It's awful hard when you lose your whole family."

"How'd you lose yours?" Noah asked.

"Car crash," Skeeter said. "Drunk driver hit them on some back road in Ohio. My older sister and her baby were with them, too."

Noah knew firsthand how Skeeter felt, but he had not lost a brother or sister and a niece or nephew at the same time he'd lost his parents. Noah wondered if the pain of that would be doubly hard. He imagined it just might be.

Skeeter sighed. "There I was, in the blink of an eye, an orphan at age eighteen. And I thought if life was that uncertain, why not throw all caution to the winds? So I joined up with the 86th. Now, like it or not, these guys are my family." He laughed ruefully.

Noah didn't say anything. The thought of replacing his mother and father with anyone, let alone a bunch of boys and men at an army base, seemed wrong.

A shout of merriment rose from around Noah's uncle.

"What's going on?" Noah asked, nodding over to where James Shelley sat surrounded. "Why is everyone so interested in my uncle?"

Skeeter paused. "You've come at a funny time. Shelley just got back from two days' leave."

"Why is everyone cheering for him?" Noah persisted.

Skeeter laughed and rubbed his fingers through his hair. "Well, it's like this. On his leave, he and another guy who's still somewhere sleeping challenged each other to a hike."

Noah shrugged. "So?" He and his father had frequently hiked into the hills near their farm to go fishing.

"They hiked from a town called Pando to Glenwood Springs," Skeeter said. "It's a distance of seventy-five miles in deep snow. They made the hike in twenty-one hours, without any sleep at all."

"That's pretty good," Noah said. The longest hike he remembered making with his father had been around ten miles.

Skeeter laughed again. "Yeah, that's pretty good. But what's even more incredible is this: See, Pete was the one who had challenged your uncle to the hike. He picked how far they would go, and he set the pace. Your uncle, though, he was responsible for the provisions on the trip." Skeeter grinned. "You know what your uncle brought?"

Noah shook his head.

"A candy bar," Skeeter hooted. "Just one candy bar. Nothing else. I guess Pete nearly died when he saw what your uncle had packed in his knapsack. The rest of it was filled with paper."

Noah thought about hiking seventy-five miles in deep snow in twenty-one hours with only half a candy bar to eat.

"That's crazy," Noah said.

"Yeah," Skeeter said, "it sure is."

Noah looked at Skeeter and saw his face shining with admiration. Then he looked at his uncle, his head thrown back, his eyes gleaming wildly out of his big, bushy face.

His uncle had taken a chance that was both foolish and dangerous. Were all soldiers like this? Or just this group that had been ridiculed by their peers? Would these soldiers do anything to prove themselves? A shiver ran down Noah's back, and he wondered just what Reverend Patterson and Mrs. Norman had gotten him into.

CHAPTER SEVEN

Skeeter loaded up a second tray with food. Then he motioned Noah to follow him back toward the others. They moved between the long, picnic-style tables until Skeeter stopped and slid the tray he was carrying onto a spot in front of James Shelley.

"Something to eat?" Skeeter asked.

Noah's uncle turned and smiled. "Much obliged, Skeeter. I'm just *slightly* hungry."

The boys around him laughed.

James Shelley grinned, then motioned them away. "Hey, I like you guys well enough, but leave a man alone to eat in peace, will ya?"

The boys all laughed again and then drifted away to the other tables.

Noah's uncle picked up his fork and began to shovel the food Skeeter had brought him into his mouth. He kept on stuffing food in until Noah was sure it would all come spilling back out.

Finally, his uncle stopped filling his mouth, chewed, and swallowed with a loud gulping noise. Abruptly, he patted the spot on the bench next to him.

"Sit, boy," he commanded.

Noah set down his tray.

"Who's the kid, Shelley?" the boy Roger yelled from across the room.

"Hitler's son!" James Shelley yelled back.

Everyone laughed again.

Then James Shelley turned to Noah. "Come on now and eat, boy. You should always eat when there's food in front of you. You never know when you may have to do without."

Noah's throat tightened to hear those words slip so easily off his uncle's tongue. His parents had said almost the exact same thing every day. Living during the worst depression the country had ever known, his parents always appreciated what they had and rarely threw anything away.

"Yes, Uncle James." Noah forced himself to respond dutifully as he sat down. He might not be fond of his uncle, but he was still family. And Noah knew his parents would have expected him to show his uncle respect.

"Shelley," his uncle said.

"What?" Noah said.

"My name's Shelley around here," his uncle said, "not James."

"All right," Noah said.

Noah took a bite of the food in front of him and immediately wanted to spit it back out. Skeeter had been right. The food was awful.

His uncle grinned. "Don't like it much, huh, boy?"

"No, sir, Uncle Shelley," Noah replied, trying to choke the food down, and yearning for his mother's cooking. Suddenly, he could smell every plate of fried chicken and okra his mother had served him over the years, every meal delivered with love and smiles.

"What'd you call me?" his uncle asked.

"Uncle Shelley," Noah said, "like you asked."

His uncle threw back his head and sent up a howl of laughter that shook the whole table. "Uncle Shelley! Uncle Shelley!"

Then he looked back at Noah and grinned. "You sure are a hoot, boy."

Noah was bewildered by his uncle's laughter. What was he supposed to call him?

James Shelley shook his head. "Yeah, you sure are." He turned and went back to eating, not saying another word until every last bite had been swallowed. Then he licked his lips and belched.

Noah shuddered. Table manners were definitely not his uncle's strong point.

"Something wrong, boy?" James Shelley asked.

Noah shook his head and stared down at his plate. He wasn't hungry anymore. There was a hard knot in his stomach.

His uncle stood and clapped Noah on the back. "Come on, then. I got to go get my mail."

Noah pushed back the plate of uneaten food and followed his uncle out of the mess hall and into the night. He was suddenly weary again.

Yet in spite of his fatigue, Noah was brought up short by the beauty of the night. Stars by the thousands lit the sky, and the air was crisp. The mountains rose, dark shadows in the distance, moonlight spilling down their sides.

James Shelley stopped, hitched up his pants, and breathed deeply. "Nothing like the mountains, boy, and the snow. You ski?"

"No, sir," Noah said, still gazing at the beauty around him.

"Never?" his uncle said, then he shook his head. "Actually, I don't know why I'm asking. I should know you'd have never skied. Our folks were strict against it 'cause of their religion. All work and no play. So, I guess your mama was, too."

"I don't know, sir," Noah said, turning his attention back to his uncle. "I never asked her. There isn't much chance to ski in Texas."

James Shelley laughed loudly. "No, I guess there wouldn't be." He shook his head. "You sure are funny, boy."

Noah shrugged. He hadn't meant to be funny at all.

His uncle began walking toward another building. He pulled open the door, and Noah followed him inside. His uncle walked up to a man sitting behind a desk. On the far wall were hundreds of metal postal boxes.

"Hey, Josh," James Shelley called. "How's it going?"

The man behind the desk looked up. "Well, if it ain't the famous Shelley, walker of the seventy-five miles." The man stood and held out his hand. "Congratulations! Glad to see you made it back in one piece."

James Shelley shook Josh's hand. "Cakewalk, really. Nothing but a stroll."

Josh shook his head. "Maybe for you, Shelley, maybe for you."

Noah's uncle laughed. "Hey, got anything for me there?"

Josh went back to the boxes and opened one. He pulled out four envelopes, turned, and handed them to Shelley before sitting back down to his work.

"Much obliged," James Shelley said. He flipped through the envelopes, finally finding one and ripping it open. He pulled out a letter.

"Well, what do you know," James Shelley said. "Says here that my nephew's on his way to stay with me awhile."

Josh looked up and then peered behind Shelley. "Looks like your nephew arrived before the mailman did, Shelley."

Noah's uncle grinned. "Good old Uncle Sam." Then he waved the envelope in the air. "Thanks, Josh." He turned to Noah. "Come on, boy. Sack time."

They walked out of the building. "Josh has the biggest mouth in camp," his uncle said. "By morning, everyone will know who you are. He's going to save me a heck of a lot of explanations."

Noah trampled along in his uncle's footsteps, painfully aware that he was unwelcome here. He didn't like the feeling. Tomorrow, Noah promised himself, he would figure out some way of getting himself back to Texas and then some way of making a living. Maybe he could hire himself out to a farmer. He dismissed this idea as soon as it came to him. He remembered how little his own parents had. No farmer from his town could afford to pay someone else to do their own work for them. They probably couldn't even afford to feed him. Still, there had to be some solution. It would just take a little time and creativity for Noah to come up with it.

Back in his uncle's barracks, Shelley handed Noah two blankets. Noah shivered. The barracks were unbelievably cold.

His uncle pointed to the bed next to his, one in a row of many beds. "You can sack out there. Cam can find some other place to sleep tonight."

Then he handed Noah a radio. "Sleep with this next to your chest. You'll need it."

"What for?" Noah asked, wrinkling his nose at the rubbery smell in the place. He thought of the sweet scents of home, the aroma of a drenching rain on hungry fields and the perfume of a Texas spring night. How could these boys stand this odor?

"You need a radio during combat," his uncle answered. "You sleep with it 'cause at night it gets cold, so cold that if you didn't sleep with it, that radio would freeze. That's just something you should learn to do. And as for the smell, which I can see is bothering you, boy, well, it smells in here from the records and candy bars we melt down to put on the bottom of our skis. It's like wax but better. It makes the skis faster. Don't worry. You'll learn all these little details tomorrow. Skeeter says you're sixteen, old enough to sign up with my permission. Heck, you should've signed up already like everybody else is doing. But being raised by pacifists, I guess not signing up isn't so strange.

But now you're with me, you might as well join the war effort here. All right, it's time for some shut-eye. Days at Camp Hell start at four thirty A.M."

His uncle smiled, seemingly happy that he had found a solution for Noah.

Noah stared at him. What had his uncle just said? He meant to sign Noah up? Was he crazy? What had Noah done, lying about being sixteen? Would he be forced to train for combat?

"Something the matter, boy?" his uncle asked.

With a great deal of effort, Noah forced the fear away and tried to think rationally. He had to stay here tonight. He had to get some sleep. But in the morning, he would tell his uncle the truth. Everything would work itself out tomorrow. Noah shook his head in answer to James Shelley's question. It was just one night. He could survive one night.

"Good," his uncle said. "Then let's get some shut-eye. I know it's early, but I'm beat. And I bet you are, too."

Noah turned and spread out his blankets on the bed.

"Uncle Shelley, sir?" he asked.

"What?" his uncle asked impatiently from his own bed.

"Can I have a pillow?" Noah asked.

His uncle shook his head. "Pillows are for softies, kid. And that's one thing we don't have here."

Then his uncle rolled over and shut off the light. The inside of the barracks was doused with darkness.

Noah slid into the bed, wrapping the blankets around him and pulling the radio tight to his chest. He thought of home longingly, of the long grasses and the flat, bright sky on a sunny day. *Tomorrow*, he reminded himself, as the strangeness of the place wrapped itself around him like a blanket of cold, *only one night and then I'll work out how to run away, what to do, and how to live by myself back home. I can do this! I can do this!*

Then softly, his uncle spoke into the darkness. "Wouldn't my old man die if he saw me now, Noah boy, you here with me and me teaching you how to ski. He hated my skiing, you know. Called me a bum, he did, my own father. He sent me away 'cause that's all I wanted to do. So I left 'cause that's all I wanted in my life, that feeling of soaring down those slopes and the wind and the snow. But the sad part was . . ."

He went silent. Noah waited, wondering if, because of the hike, his uncle had fallen asleep mid-sentence. But just when it seemed James Shelley was done talking, he started again.

"But see, the sad part was her. I had to leave her behind when he threw me out. She was only ten, and that's the last time I saw her. Yeah, that's the last time I saw your mother."

Noah turned away from his uncle. He hadn't cried once since his parents had died but the confusion and oddness of being here finally overtook him. Noah stuffed the rough blanket into his mouth so his uncle wouldn't hear the sound of the crying he could no longer prevent.

Noah needn't have worried. Within minutes, the big man next to him was snoring.

CHAPTER EIGHT

Noah woke to the sound of moaning and groaning and the sight of his uncle bending over him, shaking him awake. He rubbed his eyes, swollen slightly from the muffled tears of last night. Relief rushed through him. Today, he would leave this place.

"Rise and shine, soldiers," James Shelley sang out to everyone. "Time to get training."

Every bunk in the barracks was filled. Most of the boys were ignoring Shelley, turning over and pulling the covers back over their heads. Others were sitting on the edge of their beds and staring down at the floor. A few were actually up, but they were pulling on their pants with a bleary-eyed weariness.

Fully dressed, James Shelley was beaming. He strolled over to the door of the barracks and threw it open.

"Shelley, please," a pencil-thin boy begged. "It's cold enough in here."

"Cold's the name of the game, Cam," Noah's uncle called back, and he walked outside, leaving the door ajar.

Noah shivered. His blankets were covered in a fine layer of frost, and his breath was coming out of his mouth in white gusts.

James Shelley came back in with a bucket. "Come on, Noah boy. Let's wash up before breakfast."

Noah slid out of bed, gritting his teeth against the cold. He decided to stay in the same clothes he was wearing from the day before. He wasn't about to take the time to search his bag for something else to wear, even if it would have been cleaner.

He walked over to where his uncle stood, the bucket in front of him. His uncle handed him a bar of soap. Noah bent over and dipped his hands in the bucket, then jumped back, splashing water down his front.

The water was ice cold. "Are you kidding?" he yelled.

"Oh, come on, boy," his uncle said impatiently. "Throw some of that on yourself. It'll wake you up good."

Noah remembered the sunshine in Texas and the way the hot air pushed against his nose like a wall. He would give anything now for a touch of that warmth.

"Come on, boy," his uncle repeated, pushing Noah out of the way. "It isn't that hard." To demonstrate, James Shelley undid the top of his shirt, letting it fall down around his waist. He threw his hands into the bucket and splashed cold water all over himself, soaping up and rinsing in quick, practiced movements.

The boy named Wiley, who had had the tent pulled down on top of him, sidled up to Noah with a towel and bar of soap in his hand. "He tried to get all of us to do this on our first day here. He's crazy. Come with me, and I'll show you where you can get a good, hot shower."

James Shelley's head came up from the bucket. "What did you say?" he raged at Wiley, splashing water all around him. The boys nearby scattered to avoid getting doused. "Out! Out! Out! This is my nephew, and I'll teach him how to make his way around this camp, if you please!"

Wiley grinned at Noah. "Later," he said, winking and then running for the door.

"There'll be no later!" Shelley roared after him. "Come back here and face me, you coward!" But Wiley was already gone. Roger and Cam were silently laughing, covering their mouths to hide their mirth.

"Don't you listen to him!" James Shelley commanded Noah. "That Wiley's a softie. And no nephew of mine is gonna go soft. Got it?"

Noah nodded. Sure, he got it. He got it, loud and clear. The boy Wiley was right. His uncle was crazy. Who'd ever heard of washing in cold water when you were already freezing? Or hiking seventy-five miles with just a candy bar? These were not things a *sane* person would do.

James Shelley sighed. "Well, I guess you can skip a wash this morning. That Texas body of yours probably needs a little time to adjust to the climate around here. We'll try again tomorrow. In the meantime, let's go chow down."

His uncle grabbed up his parka and Noah did the same, following his uncle toward the mess hall. A hot breakfast, a quick talk with his uncle, and he was out of here. Noah couldn't wait.

Once they were seated with eggs and hot coffee in front of them, Noah took a deep breath. "Uncle Shelley?"

"Yeah?" his uncle said.

"Maybe my training with you isn't such a good idea."

"Why?" his uncle asked, his head coming up, his eyes shining. "You don't like it here or something?"

"No, sir," Noah lied, after seeing the fierce look on his uncle's face. "I mean, yes, sir. I mean, I like it fine, but maybe it would be better if I joined up somewhere else so you can concentrate on your work here."

James Shelley visibly relaxed at Noah's words. "Don't you concern yourself with that, boy. They can spare me for a day or two. It won't take you long to learn the routine around here. You can't go anywhere at the moment, anyway. You need authorization and a pass to take the train out, and no one's going to lend you one of the military vehicles so you can run off to another unit to sign up." His uncle laughed at the thought.

Noah's heart sank. He would need permission to take the train home?

"Yeah," his uncle said, taking a big bite of toast, "a few days' skiing and a few days' training, and you'll fit right in. Nothing to worry about, Noah boy."

Skiing? The word caught Noah's attention. He'd never even thought of skiing in Texas. The idea of learning to ski appealed to him. He'd seen pictures of people skiing.

Maybe he could take a few days to learn how to do something fun while he figured out how to get away. It would give him time to send a letter or two, to line up a job and a place to live. He really didn't have a choice. And if they started on actual combat training, he'd tell his uncle the truth about his age.

"Besides, you don't think I'd let my sister's kid just go wandering off into the world unsupervised now, do you? Come on," James Shelley said, standing and wiping his mouth with his sleeve. "Let's get you out on those slopes."

Outside, Noah followed his uncle across a central yard. The sun was just starting to rise, and the mountains were enveloped in mist. Pine trees on the lower slopes dropped large handfuls of snow to the ground with a soft plopping sound.

They entered a building filled with skiing equipment, neatly arranged from floor to ceiling. Everything but the shelves was white — the skis, the poles, the boots, and the snowshoes. The place smelled of polish and disinfectant.

"Something I can do for you, Shelley?" a man asked, rising from behind a dark wooden counter.

"I need some skis for my nephew here, Sam," James Shelley said. "I'm going to take him out for a few runs today."

"He a new recruit?" Sam asked. "I didn't know we were expecting any."

"I'd like to know the same thing," came a voice from behind them.

Noah turned to see a man in uniform, standing tall and

stern. He was the first person Noah had seen who looked as if he actually belonged in the military. His dark blue eyes bored into Noah's. The hair rose on the back of Noah's neck.

"General!" James Shelley boomed out. "I'd like you to meet my nephew, Noah Garrett."

"A pleasure, I'm sure," the general said, shaking Noah's hand. Then he turned toward Noah's uncle. "What's the story, Shelley? Why aren't you out getting ready for drills?"

Noah's uncle walked up to the general and draped his arm over the man's shoulders. "Well, it's kind of like this," he said in a low voice, turning the general back toward the door. Noah had to strain to hear him.

"He's my sister's kid," James Shelley explained. "His parents were taken with the pox. He has nowhere else to go."

The general looked severely at Noah's uncle. "Shelley, you know we can't have civilians on base."

"The kid's sixteen," James Shelley said. "His parents were pacifist types, wouldn't let him join. But Noah here had planned on joining the outfit, anyway. So, we break a little rule, and let him in without the usual routine. I mean, General, he's just like me. He can't wait to get his hands on those Germans and Japanese and prove a thing or two."

The general turned. His eyes narrowed on Noah. "Can he ski, Shelley?"

Noah didn't say anything, but he felt his palms start to sweat.

"Can he ski?" James Shelley repeated. "I mean, whose nephew is he? Of course he can ski. He's one of the best you've ever seen.

I'm just taking him out now for a little refresher. He's been in Texas lately and hasn't skied in a while."

The general shook a finger at Noah's uncle. "If you're pulling a fast one on me, Shelley, I swear I'll bring you up on charges."

James Shelley smiled at the general, his eyes wide and innocent. "What? You don't believe me?"

Noah watched the exchange in disbelief as his uncle lied without even twitching.

The general sighed. "Oh, all right. For you, Shelley, 'cause you're one of the best here. And because in this godforsaken place, I guess it won't get back to headquarters about him, just like they don't know that you guys don't ever march or wear uniforms."

He paused. "But, Shelley, I'm warning you. In eight weeks, we're having a drill, and if I don't see that kid skiing his heart out, he's on his way back to wherever he came from. You get me his papers. I want that kid's birth certificate and three letters of recommendation on my desk, pronto. I want your signed approval for him to join up since you're his guardian, and he's under eighteen. And you're back on training tomorrow. From what I've heard, you've already had a few days off. Is that understood?"

"Yes, sir," Noah's uncle said, standing straight and saluting the general.

The general waved his hand at Shelley. "Aw, cut the crap. Nobody else around here shows me any sign of respect. Why should you?"

Then, turning on his heel, the general was gone.

James Shelley turned to face Noah. "You're gonna learn to ski, boy, and you're gonna learn to do it quick."

Noah felt his face flush. Now three people believed he was sixteen. Would the numbers grow until Noah could no longer back out gracefully and admit he'd lied? Would he get himself and his uncle into real trouble just because he wanted to have a little fun?

It was too late to think about that now. What was done was done. He might as well have a good time. So Noah pushed the worry from his mind, picked up the skis and poles, and followed his uncle out the door.

CHAPTER NINE

Noah and his uncle climbed the side of one of the mountains in their ski boots until they were at the top of a very long slope. Below him, Noah could see the other boys and their officers, skiing out and away from them, toward another mountain. Mules, loaded down with equipment, plodded along behind the soldiers.

Noah's feet and hands were already numb with cold, but his heart was pounding with excitement. His uncle bent down and gathered some snow, squeezing it into a hard clump. Then he stood and rummaged around in his rucksack, finally pulling out a small metal container.

"Here, boy," Shelley commanded, handing the tube to him. "This is ski wax. You can start by rubbing this on the bottom of your skis. We use different types of wax depending on the weather."

He showed Noah how to apply the wax to the bottom of the wooden skis he had requisitioned for him. The wax was warm and smooth to the touch and slid on easily.

When Noah finished with the waxing, his uncle took the boards, knelt down, and showed Noah how to attach them to his leather boots. Then his uncle stood and stepped back.

Noah grinned and took a step forward, swayed a bit, tried adjusting, and fell hard.

His uncle let out a loud laugh. "Your balance ain't too good, boy."

Noah frowned, the excitement of learning to ski lessening slightly with the embarrassment of falling so incredibly quickly and the uncomfortable feeling of the seat of his pants growing suddenly wet and cold. "My balance is just fine, sir. It's the skis that are the problem."

His uncle laughed even harder. "Oh, that's a good one, Noah boy."

"It wasn't a joke," Noah said angrily, wanting his uncle to stop saying how funny he was when he wasn't trying to be funny.

His uncle stopped laughing. "No, I guess it wasn't. Here, let's try again."

He pulled Noah to his feet and held him still until he was sure Noah was balanced. Then he turned to put on his own skis.

Noah felt awkward just standing there, afraid to move. In the pictures he'd seen, skiing had looked easy, but the long wooden boards strapped to his feet made Noah feel unwieldy. He shifted his weight to try and get more comfortable, but as he did so, the skis suddenly started to slide out from under him. And he began to move down the slope.

"Turn your skis into the hill," his uncle cried out as he saw Noah begin to slip down the mountain. "Into the hill, boy!"

Noah tried to pound the skis into the snow on the mountain as his uncle had instructed, but instead, he began to pick up speed.

"Help!" Noah managed to shout through the fear that was now thick in his throat.

His skis were moving quickly, as if they had a life of their own, and Noah was in their control. He wavered back and forth, as the world flew by. He leaned backward, trying to stop himself any way he could, and then his knees buckled. He sat straight down onto the skis, and the skis kept going like a toboggan racing down the hill. Snow flew everywhere. Pine trees blurred together as he hurtled down the slope.

Noah put his hands out to stop himself. He tumbled forward over and over, down the side of the hill until finally, he came to a stop. He was on his back, his legs spread apart, the skis pointing in opposite directions. Amazingly, nothing seemed broken, yet Noah was shocked by how fast the skis had made him go.

There was a loud swishing sound, and his uncle came flying up beside him. He stopped suddenly, sending a spray of snow into Noah's face and laughing so hard his cheeks were beet red.

"I wish you could have seen yourself, Noah boy," his uncle cried. "You were all legs and arms, kid. They were going every which way."

His uncle laughed again. Noah glared up at him, swung one leg over to meet the other, and tried to stand. But the skis wouldn't let him. They kept slipping away again.

"How about some help?" Noah finally grumbled to his uncle.

His uncle shook his head. "That's the first lesson in skiing, and one you'll have to learn by yourself, boy. If you're ever out skiing alone, you'll have to know how to stand without help if you should fall."

Noah gritted his teeth. How was he supposed to do that on his own? It was impossible with these big boards on his feet!

Still, he did as his uncle instructed and tried to get himself up. But just as he came almost to standing, he started to slide down the hill again. Immediately, Noah was back on the ground.

"Turn the skis into the hill, boy," his uncle said, bending down and showing Noah how to turn the skis parallel to the slope. "Like this. See?"

Then he handed Noah his poles. "Now, try again, using these."

Noah dug the poles into the snow and tried to push himself up. His arms collapsed under his weight.

"Gotta build up those muscles, it looks like," his uncle said. "Don't exercise much, huh?"

Noah looked up at his uncle. "I exercised, sir. I farmed and fished. I had a lot of chores to do. Those chores were hard work."

His uncle snorted. "Don't I remember! Your mom and I grew up on a farm not too far from here. All that farm work was so boring. I used to sneak off, though, with these old skis I'd found in somebody's trash that I fixed up and hid in these mountains, and I'd ski my heart out. Bet you wanted to do the same thing, huh, Noah boy?"

"Not really, sir," Noah said. "I lived in Texas, remember?"

"Ah, you just haven't got a feel for fun yet," his uncle said. "Come on. Try getting up again. You're going to have to do this a lot today. And then tomorrow, I'll get Daniel Stultz to teach you. He's a darn good little skier for a kid from the Bronx. I've got to get back to military matters myself."

Noah pushed and pushed and finally managed to get himself up. Then his uncle showed him how to attach small, narrow sealskins to the bottom of his skis to help with the climb back up the side of the mountain. Noah shuddered as he attached the skins, the small hairs soft to the touch when you brushed them one way, prickly when you brushed them the other. Noah wondered how many seals had been killed so that skiers might find an easier way up the mountain.

The skins grabbed the snow, preventing the skis from slipping downhill. Still, Noah could feel his heart pounding fiercely in his chest and sweat running down his back with each step he took.

When at last they reached the top of the hill, Noah's uncle turned and smiled. "Don't worry, boy. Forty or fifty more times of this, and you'll ski like a pro for that general." Then his uncle threw back his head and laughed once more.

The rest of the day was a blur to Noah, a blur of snow: in his face, down his pants, in his gloves, in his eyes. Over and over again, they went down the hill. Each time Noah fell, he struggled to get himself standing again and climb back up the mountain.

When they returned to the barracks, Noah's hands shook as he unlaced his leather ski boots. Every part of his body ached beyond belief. Never from all the work he had done around the farm had he been this tired.

"Bet you're ready for a good meal, boy," his uncle said, taking the boots from him.

Noah didn't answer. He just slumped forward onto his bed and fell fast asleep.

When he woke, it was dark. Noah turned over. Someone had pulled a blanket up around him, and for once, he felt warm. And then he noticed a pillow under his head. He wanted to thank whoever had given it to him, but he felt too weak to move.

He heard a door open and the sound of footsteps.

"How is he?" came a soft voice. It was Skeeter.

"Still sleeping," his uncle whispered.

"I brought you some dinner."

"Set it down by the boy's bed, if you don't mind," James Shelley said. "He may wake and be hungry tonight."

Noah heard the clink of glass and silverware close by. He could smell the sweet aroma of food, but he was too tired to roll over and sit up to eat. It was too warm, too easy just lying there without saying a word.

"How'd he do today?" Skeeter asked.

"Good," his uncle said. "He done real good. He was able to snowplow at the end."

Noah drifted back to sleep as Skeeter and Shelley talked in low tones. Then he heard his name and was pulled back awake.

"I got some info for you, Shelley. A response came in an hour or so ago from that minister with an answer to your telegram. The kid's only fifteen."

Noah held still, not wanting them to know he was awake. His ears strained to hear what they were saying in the dark of the bunkroom.

James Shelley whistled softly. "Great. What am I going to do? There's no other place for him to go, and I won't put my sister's kid in no orphanage."

There was a silence.

"Maybe this little piece of information should stay between us, huh, Skeeter?" James Shelley finally said.

"But what if we get shipped out?" Skeeter asked.

"I don't know," Shelley said. "I can't think that far ahead."

"He'll have to go through combat training." Skeeter's voice was worried. "If we say he's sixteen, they'll make him act sixteen."

"Well, he lied to us about his age, so now that's his age. Besides, a little hard work never hurt nobody." James Shelley chuckled. "It'll be good punishment for the lying."

Skeeter chuckled, too. Then they were quiet again.

"Think we can pull it off?" Skeeter whispered.

"I hope so," Noah's uncle replied.

"You getting attached to that boy, Shelley?" Skeeter asked.

There was a pause. "I ain't never been attached to no one, Skeeter, and don't you forget it."

"Right, Shelley," Skeeter said.

Noah heard footsteps walking away and a door opening and

closing. Then he heard the creak of a chair being dragged toward his bed. His uncle sat down heavily and did not move.

Noah knew that he should be worried that he'd been found out. He knew that he should be upset about maybe having to face combat training, with possibly no way to stop it. But he was too tired to think about that now.

His uncle sat beside him without saying a word. And Noah fell right back asleep.

CHAPTER TEN

Noah could barely turn over when his uncle shook him awake the next morning. Every inch of him ached.

"You have to have a bath today, Noah boy." His uncle's voice boomed out above him. "Don't want any smelly bodies in my barracks." Then he was gone and out the door.

Noah pushed himself out of bed by rolling onto his knees. His arms couldn't support him. How was he supposed to go and ski again today? The very idea gave him a headache. He wouldn't do it. He couldn't. Not without a hot shower at the very least.

Noah moved painfully between the bunks until he reached the boy who had offered to show him where the showers were yesterday morning.

Wiley grinned at Noah with slightly crooked teeth. "Ready to join the sane ones, huh?"

Noah nodded.

James Shelley came flying back into the barracks, his ice bucket slopping water all around. "Okay, Noah, bath time."

Noah looked at the ice water in the bucket. "No, sir."

The barracks suddenly grew still.

The boy, Roger, let out a slight whistle.

"What did you say?" Noah's uncle asked, his voice low and threatening.

Noah felt a shiver run down his back. In all his years, he had never said a direct "no" to his mother or father, though he'd wanted to enough times. It just wasn't the way he'd been raised. But Noah was too tired and too worried to care anymore. His whole body cried out for a hot shower, and he felt that if he didn't get one, he would break down, in front of all these soldiers. The idea was too embarrassing to even consider.

"I said no, sir," Noah repeated, lifting his chin a little.

Noah could hear the boys draw in their breath and watched their eyes turn back to James Shelley. The big man stared so long at Noah that he began to feel his courage ebbing away.

Then, in one quick step, his uncle was by Noah's side, taking him by the arm and pulling him roughly away from the others.

"No, no, boy," his uncle whispered in a harsh tone when they were out of earshot of the others. "Don't you dare change your mind now!"

Noah blinked. Had he heard his uncle right?

"I can see those little wheels turning," his uncle continued, "and I can see you're feeling bad about standing up for what you believe in. It's 'cause of all that polite stuff you were raised on. Well, don't you do it. You want a hot shower, then say you want a hot shower. And don't let me or any other man bully you into doing what you don't want to. You said no. Now stick by your decision and forget about it. That's the proud and right thing to do, Noah Garrett. Be your own man."

Then his uncle turned from him and went back to the bucket and began to wash his face. Noah was so shocked, he didn't move or say a word.

His uncle turned to them all, a towel in his hands. "Noah, if you're going to the showers, then get going! Now! And what are the rest of you big blockheads doing there, staring at me like that? Get dressed! We've got maneuvers today! And not one of you had better even entertain the idea that because that boy is going to the showers, I've grown soft. No way! The rest of you will do as I say and like it. I will entertain no arguments! Now get moving!"

The barracks was a sudden flurry of movement. Wiley touched Noah on the shoulder. "Come on. Let me show you where the showers are."

The hot water felt like heaven as Noah let it pound on his aching shoulders, arms, and back. But with the luxury of hot water came the memory of the conversation he'd overheard last night.

What was he supposed to do now? His uncle knew his age and was willing to let Noah go through combat training to keep the secret. How could he stop this insanity? Tears slipped down his cheeks and blended in with the water from the shower. Noah let the tears fall. At least here, no one would see him break down.

Then a face popped up over the wooden wall next to him. Noah quickly turned his head away so Wiley wouldn't see him crying. Wiley switched on the shower in his own stall, the hot water sending puffs of steam into the air.

"Aw, now," Wiley said, "don't be embarrassed. You should have seen me bawling like a baby in these very same showers the afternoon I came back from my first day skiing out here. I made such a waterfall, they had to call the flood patrol out."

Noah couldn't help it. He laughed and turned back to face Wiley, wiping his eyes. The boy's freckled face was an orb of goodwill.

"Nah," Wiley continued, "it ain't easy here, that's for sure. But man, I'll take training with these guys any old day compared to being in the unit my brothers are in."

"Your brothers are signed up, too?" Noah asked.

Wiley rolled his eyes. "Signed up? We were born into the military — all of us. My father was in the army. He's stationed in London right now. Two of my brothers are somewhere off the coast of France with their naval units. And my sister is in the Women's Army Auxiliary Corps. And as for my mother . . ."

Here, he paused and grinned again. "She *ought* to be in the military the way she can yell and boss us around like some tough old drill sergeant." He looked thoughtful for a moment. "But she's a lovable sergeant at that."

Noah smiled.

"Look, it'll be hard going for a while," Wiley told him, turning and picking up a bar of soap, "but then one day, you'll wake up and you'll be all fit and relaxed and you won't believe how good you'll look. It's a fine feeling when that day comes. So hold on for it. Where you from, by the by?"

"Texas," Noah answered.

"Texas?" Wiley said, his eyes widening. "How the Sam Hill you learn to ski in Texas? I ain't the best in geography, but I don't remember no mountains in Texas."

Noah looked carefully at Wiley. He liked the boy's open look and his humor. He'd never had a close friend before, but strangely, he felt that Wiley could be one.

"Can I tell you a secret?" Noah asked him.

"Well, sure. You can trust me," Wiley said, pausing in his soaping up.

"I've actually never skied before," Noah whispered. "And the general swore I had to be skiing as well as the rest of you in eight weeks, or I was out of here."

Wiley let out a loud guffaw, shocking Noah.

"Oh man, you've got to relax," Wiley said, rubbing shampoo deep into his hair. "Half the officers in this unit can't ski worth a hill of beans. And the other are so wild about the sport, they got no military discipline at all. They're desperate for recruits. You look athletic enough. A day or two more, you'll be skiing good enough. I'm sure of it."

He rinsed the shampoo from his hair and then stuck his hand over the stall wall. "We ain't been properly introduced. My name's Wiley Evans. I'm from New Hampshire. Been with these guys about nine months now."

"Noah Garrett," Noah said, enthusiastically shaking Wiley's hand, grateful for his encouragement.

"Was that tent pulled down around you while you were training here?" Noah asked, referring to the story he'd heard on his first night at Camp Hale.

Wiley laughed again and shook his head. "Nah, that was in Kiska, Alaska, one of them Aleutian Islands. Some of us boys were sent up there to rid the island of Japanese who'd invaded it awhile back. It was the first time out for a lot of us, so we weren't real smart about setting up tents in the wind."

"Did you see any Japanese?" Noah asked, surprised at the casualness with which Wiley referred to his first time in combat.

"Not a one," Wiley said. "They'd slipped past the U.S. of A.'s estimable navy in the fog, and by the time we got there, they were long gone. 'Course that didn't prevent us from scouring the island ourselves, trying to find them and frightening ourselves silly each time we ran into one another. We kept thinking those Japanese were holed up somewhere and about to pop out at us."

"Sounds scary," Noah said without thinking, feeling himself blush as he said it. Would Wiley think he was a coward?

Wiley guffawed again. "You got that right. I almost crapped my pants half the time."

Just then, Noah heard the door to the barracks open and his uncle's voice calling his name.

"Over here, Uncle Shelley," Noah shouted back.

His uncle came and stood by the shower stall. "You going to stay in there all day or what?"

Noah turned off the water and stepped out, wrapping a towel around himself. Wiley's words had given Noah back his confidence. He was sure, now that he was warmed and showered, his muscles relaxed, that he could take on the skiing today without a problem.

"Well, boy," his uncle said, "let's get you on over to Daniel Stultz. He'll be taking you out."

Wiley let out a long whistle. "Not cutting your nephew any slack, eh, Shelley?"

Noah's uncle glared at Wiley. "You got him his shower, Wiley. You'd best not mess with me again."

"Wouldn't dream of it," Wiley said, grinning.

"Who's Daniel Stultz?" Noah asked, as he pulled on his pants.

Wiley stepped out of the shower, too, toweling himself off. "Just the best ski instructor in the unit, and the toughest, on himself and everybody else around him."

"How much tougher can it get?" Noah asked.

"With Daniel Stultz?" Wiley said with an edge of contempt in his voice. "You survive a day with Mr. Gloomy, they ought to give you the Medal of Honor."

"That's enough, Wiley!" Noah's uncle suddenly snapped. "Daniel's a part of this unit, and an officer. I'll expect you to show him the same respect you show your other fellow soldiers. Is that understood?"

Wiley blinked with surprise, all the joking now gone. "Yes, sir." He turned away to put on his pants, but Noah saw the color rise in his face.

Noah felt sorry for Wiley being reprimanded so harshly right in front of him, but he could think of nothing to say to smooth things over.

"Get dressed now, Noah," his uncle commanded, a roughness in his voice. "I've got to get to maneuvers."

Noah scrambled to put on his shirt, fumbling with the buttons. "What will I be doing today with Daniel?"

"Nothing you can't handle, boy," James Shelley responded firmly. "Nothing you can't do."

CHAPTER ELEVEN

The campground was a flurry of activity as officers and soldiers ran around preparing for the day's training. Mules brayed loudly amid the confusion. Noah walked behind his uncle, trying to still the nervousness he felt.

Back at the barracks, his uncle ordered him to grab his skis and poles and put on his ski boots, a wool hat and gloves, and wool ski pants. Then they were out the door, into a jeep, and driving a few miles from camp until they stood at the bottom of another mountain where a rope with upside-down metal Ts scaled the side.

"What's that?" Noah asked, looking at the strange contraption as he stepped out of the jeep.

"A T-bar," James Shelley said. "The next step in your training."

"Do they provide those in war?" Noah joked.

For the first time since he'd arrived, Noah was trying to be funny, but his uncle did not laugh. "No, but using a T-bar means you'll get back up the mountain faster, which means you'll ski down a lot more times than you did yesterday."

Noah felt his heart sink. More times than yesterday? Was it possible to be more exhausted than he had been last night?

The sound of skis on snow sounded behind them. A young man who looked to be in his mid to late twenties glided up beside them, his white parka, pants, boots, and skis contrasting starkly with his dark skin, dark hair, and dark, brooding eyes. He lowered the white scarf he had around his mouth and stared at Noah with disapproval.

"Daniel," his uncle said, "this is my nephew, Noah Garrett. He ain't much to look at and he's got a long way to go physically, but he'll listen to you and follow your instructions, won't you, boy?"

Noah decided it was best not to challenge his uncle in front of others twice in one day. "Yes, sir."

"I don't like this, Shelley," Daniel spoke up. "Taking time to train someone who has no skiing experience whatsoever isn't a good thing for this division. We're past that now. I should be out with the rest of you, getting my unit ready for combat."

"He's family, Daniel," James Shelley said. "I thought you, of all people, would understand."

Daniel Stultz turned and looked up at the mountainside. Finally, he nodded. "Fine, but he had better work his heart out. Otherwise it's a waste of my day."

"Wouldn't expect anything less of him," James Shelley said. He turned toward Noah. "You heard him, boy. Work your heart out today!"

Noah sighed. Did he have a choice?

James Shelley drove away, and Noah was left with Daniel Stultz, who promptly skied over and switched on a metal toggle near the closest T-bar. Immediately, an engine began to hum and the metal Ts started to move up the mountain.

"Hey, what's powering that thing?" Noah asked, delighted and curious.

"A car engine," Daniel responded. "Perhaps you'd rather work in the mechanical division of this unit? If so, we can leave off teaching you to ski, and I can get back to training for war."

The man's abruptness startled Noah. After all, he'd just asked a simple question. Noah shook his head, feeling as if he had been reprimanded as harshly as Wiley had been that morning.

"Let's get to work, then," Daniel said. "I'm going to show you how to rest against the metal Ts to let them pull you up the mountain. I'm only going to show you once, so you'd better pay attention."

Noah put his skis on, then followed Daniel over to the T-bar, resentment building inside him. Who did this guy think he was?

Daniel stepped nearer the metal Ts that floated past. "When you think you're ready, step into line with the Ts. When one comes near you, set yourself on it and lean back, but not too far back. Just rest easy and let it slide you up the mountain."

Noah watched as Daniel stepped over and leaned back against the metal T that swung toward him. He watched the contraption pull Daniel up the slope a short distance. Then Daniel let go, stepped away, and skied back down to Noah. He made everything look simple. And Noah knew in that moment that Daniel was one of those boys to whom everything came easily, someone who could perform every act of athleticism with grace.

"Now you try," Daniel commanded.

Noah stepped up to the T-bar and waited for the next metal T to reach him. As he felt it hit him from behind, he sat down. Before he knew it, he was on the ground, flat on his back.

"Get up," Daniel said, rolling his eyes. "Try again, and don't lean so far back this time."

Feeling humiliated, Noah got up and sidestepped back into line with the T-bar. For the second time, he stood until he felt the metal hit his behind, then he leaned as easily on it as he could. The T-bar began to pull him up the slope, and Noah shouted with excitement. Then suddenly his skis crossed over each other and tripped him up. His ankle turned slightly on him, and he let out a yelp of pain as he was thrown to the ground.

Daniel came sliding up the mountain and stepped out next to Noah. "Well, at least you're up the mountain a bit, so you might as well try skiing down. And next time you use the tow, concentrate on keeping your skis straight."

Noah pushed himself up off the ground, his ankle aching in protest. Without another word, he gently snowplowed his way down the short slope, the way his uncle had taught him yesterday.

Noah went over to the T-bar once more, determined to show Daniel that he, Noah Garrett, was a fast learner.

This time, he was successful. Triumph surged through him as he rode farther and farther up the mountain. Then, abruptly, he was at the top. He saw the rope moving toward a pulley that flipped both it and the metal bars back down the mountain.

"What do I do?" Noah shouted out to Daniel. "What do I do now?"

There was no time. The end was there. Noah let go in a panic. Without the T pulling him forward and with his skis pointed directly up the mountain, Noah began to slide backward. He tried to turn his skis sideways to the mountain, but instead, they swung him around and threw him directly into the T-bar cable. Noah found himself on the ground once more.

Daniel came riding up the slope. "Move out of the way."

Noah scooted his butt away from the towline, and Daniel swung himself casually off and sidestepped his way toward Noah.

"Get up," he commanded. "Ski down, and try again."

"You didn't tell me what to do when I got to the end," Noah said angrily. "Why didn't you explain to me what to do?"

"Do you honestly think someone will be there to tell you what to do in the midst of a battle?" Daniel asked, his eyes snapping with a strange, barely controlled rage. "Use your brain, Garrett. You saw me step away from the T-bar earlier. You should have made a mental note of it. War is not for sissies. No one's going to hold your hand over there. Get used to it!"

"I'm just learning!" Noah protested, bewildered at Daniel's anger. "Don't you think you could give me a little advice, at least on the first time?"

Daniel gave a short bark of a laugh. "Sure, Noah. How about this for advice? 'We are what we repeatedly do. Excellence, then, is not an act, but a habit.' Aristotle. Does that explain anything to you?"

Noah said nothing, but he was seething inside.

Daniel crossed his arms across his chest. "So, now let's start working on your skiing technique and see if we can't bring you to excellence. You won't be able to snowplow down mountains when we finally go into action. You're too slow!"

Reluctantly, Noah stood up and headed back down the mountain, all the while listening to Daniel's sharp voice instructing him how to parallel ski while barely concealing his disgust. Noah had no idea what this man's problem was, but he knew one thing: Daniel Stultz definitely had one.

CHAPTER TWELVE

Noah stumbled back to the barracks, his arms aching and his legs trembling with fatigue. He hurled his skis and poles into the corner and made his way to his bunk, throwing himself down on the bed and covering his eyes with one arm. What a disaster the day had been! He had gone up and down that stupid mountain at least a hundred times with only one quick break for some hot coffee that still had the grounds in it and a stone-cold sandwich on stale bread.

"Problem, Garrett?" Daniel had asked as he complacently swallowed part of his sandwich as if it were the best thing he had ever tasted. "Perhaps you think the army will be providing you with caviar and champagne during battle?"

"How about giving a guy a break?" Noah said.

"A break?" Daniel said, "In life, you need to make your own breaks, Garrett. You have to fight harder, study longer, and work better than anyone else to get what you want. No one's going to hand it to you."

"You sure won't," Noah muttered as he swallowed the rest of the coffee, trying not to choke on the grounds. At least the coffee was hot.

The worst of it was that the food had been the *best* part of the day. Even as Noah began to grow weary, Daniel didn't let up on him, making him practice parallel turning over and over and over.

"You think those Germans are going to give you time to rest in between attacks?" Daniel had asked, as Noah paused a moment before using the T-bar again.

"Probably more time than you have," Noah said.

"Perhaps your uncle and the general would like to know your kindly opinion of our enemies," Daniel said, his voice as cold as the air around them. "If you think for one moment that I'm tougher on you than the Germans will be, then you are dumber than you look. Of course, I probably shouldn't worry. A lot of you guys just up and quit. You seem like a quitter to me, Garrett."

Noah turned, his hands balled into fists. "Do you really think I care what *you* think of me?" he said through clenched teeth, feeling such anger, it almost shocked him.

Daniel was unfazed. "I'm not here for a popularity contest, Garrett. I am your supervisor, and as such, I will have your respect, whether you like me or not. In the meantime, get skiing. This conversation has wasted enough of my time already."

Thinking back on what had happened today, Noah decided

Daniel Stultz was right about one thing. For once in his life, he *would* be a quitter, and that was fine by him. He'd wasted enough of his own time, too, with this foolish idea of learning to ski. It was time for action.

Just then, Wiley; Roger; the thin boy, Cam; and another boy with brown hair that drooped into his green eyes came through the door.

"Hey there, Noah," Wiley called out. "Looks like Mr. Gloomy worked you over good today, eh?"

Noah sat up slowly, trying to ignore the pain shooting through his body. "That would be an understatement."

The whole crowd laughed.

The boy with the green eyes held out his hand. "Bill Hanson."

Noah shook his hand. "Noah Garrett."

Cam and Roger introduced themselves, too.

"Don't let Daniel Stultz get to you," Bill said as he sat down to take off his ski boots. "He's always angry and mean-spirited. He was born that way."

"Yeah," Roger said as he plopped down on his bunk. "That's why we call him Mr. Gloomy — or my favorite, Dour Dan."

The others laughed good-naturedly. Noah joined them. It felt good to know that the others didn't like Daniel, either.

The boys peeled off their skiing clothes, washed up, and changed.

"Can't you guys hurry up?" Cam complained. "I'm starving."

"You're always starving, Kramer," Roger said to Cam. "It's amazing they have any food left in the state of Colorado the way you eat."

"You want to join us for dinner in the mess hall, Noah?" Wiley asked as he pulled on his jacket.

Noah nodded. It would be nice to be with people who weren't barking orders at him all the time. "Sure. I'll join you in just a few minutes. I've got to make a quick stop at the mail room first."

Noah changed into clean clothes, too. His skiing outfit reeked of sweat and hard work.

He dug around in his rucksack to see how much money he had. It wasn't much. It certainly wouldn't get him all the way back to Texas, but there was enough there to make a start. If he knew he had a job waiting for him, he'd ride as far as he could and then hitchhike the rest of the way home.

He grabbed up a few pennies and hobbled back out into the cold, making his way across the camp and nodding to other soldiers who were heading in to dinner. He opened the door to the building his uncle had taken him to that first night.

Josh, the mail room clerk, looked up and grinned. "Hey there. Shelley's nephew, right?"

Noah nodded.

"Well, boy, I hope you ain't looking for anything just yet," Josh said. "It usually takes the good old U.S. of A.'s mail system a few weeks to get letters to its new recruits."

Noah shook his head. "Actually, I wanted to send off a letter myself."

"No problem," Josh said. "Just give it to me, and I'll put it in the post."

"I need to write it first," Noah said. "Do you happen to have paper and an envelope?"

"Sure do." Josh reached under the counter and handed the items to Noah. He nodded his head toward a table and chairs. "You can sit over there if you want."

Noah sat down and began his letter to Reverend Patterson, imploring the minister to try and find some place for Noah to work, some way to get him get out of this situation. The warmth of the mail office eased his tired muscles. As he wrote, he remembered clearly how it felt after a day working in the fields with his father: the strain of unhooking the plow, the warmth of the horse's flanks as he led him to his stall, the cold of the water from the pump outside his house. He remembered standing there with his dad, letting the water run over both their heads and down their necks, feeling the chill as the wind blew across the land. He remembered looking up to see the red of the sun setting through a bank of rain clouds and smelling the first scent of warm pie coming from the kitchen. Noah was so wrapped up in the memory that he almost didn't notice Josh near him. When he did, he quickly covered the letter.

Josh gave a bark of laughter. "Got a girl back home, boy?"

"No, sir," Noah answered, trying not to scowl at the man's nosiness.

"Must be someone important you're writing to, to make you so cautious," Josh said, grinning.

"It's no one," Noah said. "No one important."

"Then why waste the three cents?" Josh asked.

"Don't you have something else to do?" Noah snapped.

Josh held up his hands. "Whoa, sorry. Didn't mean to rile you. Just making conversation, trying to get to know you a little, that's all. Forget I asked."

He turned and went back to the counter.

Noah sighed. He shouldn't have bitten the man's head off, but he didn't want it getting back to his uncle that he'd written Reverend Patterson. He finished the letter, addressed it, and licked the envelope shut. Reluctantly, he carried it over to Josh.

"I'm sorry," Noah said as he handed him the letter. "I'm just tired tonight."

Josh nodded. "Sure. I understand."

He glanced down at the address. "Hey, your uncle just telegraphed this guy yesterday. Nothing's wrong, is it?"

Noah grimaced. There was no way of getting around it now. His uncle would know about the letter. He'd have to think up some excuse for writing Reverend Patterson.

"No," Noah said as he paid Josh the three cents for a stamp, "he's just a friend."

Noah headed back outside. He was no longer hungry. The memory of home and the time with his parents hung like an icy blanket over him. He wanted his parents to be there with him again. He wanted to be home instead of at this military base, training for a war with scowling, shouting men who were on a mission he didn't believe in and had no intention of becoming a part of.

But Noah knew this was his reality, at least for the time being. And the thought exhausted him.

He made his way back to his barracks. The idea of dinner with Wiley and the others, in spite of their kindness, was too much to bear. He just couldn't sit there tonight and laugh and joke. There was nothing funny about the way he was feeling.

He opened the door to find Skeeter sitting on his bunk. "I was waiting for you," Skeeter told him. "Your uncle is on night maneuvers. I told him I'd watch out for you."

"I can look after myself," Noah said tightly, thinking about the fact that his uncle had thought it funny that he was to go through this ordeal.

"There's a Ping-Pong championship in the mess hall after dinner," Skeeter said. "What do you say we grab some chow and go watch?"

"I'm not hungry," Noah said, sitting down next to Skeeter. "And I'm too sore to watch a dumb old game."

"Tough going today?" Skeeter asked.

Noah shrugged.

Skeeter stared out at the rows of bunks for a minute or two. "You know, before Camp Hale was built, we were stationed at Fort Lewis near Mount Rainier. My first days with the outfit were awful. I remember sitting there after hours of training wondering what the heck I had gotten myself into."

Noah didn't respond. Sure, he hated the training, but worse, he hated the loss of all he had known. He thought about telling Skeeter that was the real problem, but he just didn't have the heart to tonight.

Skeeter gave a little laugh and went on in spite of Noah's lack of response. "So there I was, a former *ski* captain at Harvard, so confident and full of myself. I had been so sure I was going to show those boys of the 86th a thing or two. I got to Fort Lewis and remember looking up at Mount Rainier and thinking, 'You're mine!' I was determined to climb that mountain faster and better than anyone ever had before. And then some Finnish resistance fighters arrived to train us and the guys from Norway who'd been battling those Germans showed up to teach us a thing or two. And I suddenly learned just how sadly lacking I was."

"*I* never told anyone *I* had any skills at all," Noah said bitterly.

"I didn't mean that, Noah," Skeeter said. "I know you didn't sign up for this. I know this isn't what you wanted. I know what's making you hurt right now, and it isn't the soreness."

Noah looked at Skeeter.

"It's the homesickness, kid," Skeeter said. "For me, too, that was the *hardest* thing of all. There I was, literally beating my body into submission, trying through hard work and exhaustion to forget all that sadness over my parents and sister being gone. But every morning when I woke, the first thing I thought about was home. I longed for the smell of an Ohio spring. I longed for the sound of my parents' soft voices coming in through the screen door from our front porch on a summer's evening. I longed for just one more . . ." Skeeter's voice grew raspy, and he had to stop to swallow. ". . . one more day with them . . . just one."

Noah looked away, his own throat tight. Skeeter did understand.

"That longing, Noah, it won't ever go away," Skeeter said, standing. "It'll lessen somewhat, and you'll learn to live with it. But it's a part of who you are now." He paused. "And I learned one other thing those early days training with these guys at Mount Rainier."

Noah looked up.

"You can't run from the human race, son. Eventually, you've got to give up trying to escape and join in again." Skeeter walked to the front of the barracks and opened the door. "So, what do you say? Shall we give it a go?"

Noah bit his lip. Maybe Skeeter was right. He couldn't just keep sulking day in and day out. He had to start somewhere. He stood.

Together, Skeeter and he walked in silence across the camp. And when Skeeter opened the door to the mess hall, Wiley looked up and broke into a wide grin.

"Hey!" he called. "What took you so dang long? Thought you'd *never* get here. Come on now. Grab some food. And we're taking bets on the game. You want to place a wager?"

The others, too, looked up at him expectantly.

"Go on, boy," Skeeter said. "Take the first step."

"Skeeter?" Noah asked, pausing for a moment. "Did you ever get to the top of Mount Rainier?"

"I did, boy," Skeeter assured him. "I surely did."

CHAPTER THIRTEEN

That night, Noah ate dinner with Wiley, Cam, Roger, and Bill. He played cards with them, and even went ten rounds in the Ping-Pong tournament, almost making it to the finals, which endeared him to his bunkmates, who now saw him as the "barracks hero." The best part of the evening had been the boys cheering him on, while over in a corner, Daniel Stultz sat alone, reading a book, not a friend in sight.

The next morning, Noah woke weary, but less sore than he had been the morning before. He showered and dressed, his muscles loosening quickly.

When Daniel came into the barracks, Wiley gave a "*heil* Hitler" sign behind his back. Noah had to try hard not to laugh.

"Today's our last day together," Daniel said, plopping a rucksack down next to Noah. "Olaf will be taking over your training tomorrow."

Noah kept his eyes on the floor, knowing a look of relief was crossing his face.

"So, today we conquer the hard part," Daniel said. "And you'll be out there until you've mastered it."

The hard part? Noah thought, raising his head in alarm.

"It's one thing to ski, Garrett," Daniel Stultz said. "It's another to ski with eighty pounds strapped to your back."

Noah glanced at the empty rucksack. "That hardly looks like eighty pounds."

"Of course it's not eighty pounds yet," Daniel snapped. "But believe me, Garrett, it will be by the time you finish packing it up."

Daniel wasn't joking. He had Noah fill that rucksack until it was bulging, stuffing in a tent, a sleeping bag, clothes, ammunition, some food, and a real stove with the gas to light it. By the time they were finished, Noah couldn't even lift the thing.

"How am I supposed to get this up and onto my back?" Noah asked.

Daniel shrugged. "Your problem, Garrett. But I don't think the Germans will come over and help you out."

"My fellow soldiers might," Noah pointed out testily.

"Not if you're on patrol by yourself," said Daniel.

Noah looked at the rucksack, lying there on the floor. An idea came to him. He lay down on his back and slipped his arms through the pack straps. He tried to sit, but quickly fell over.

Finally, he rolled over on his stomach and pushed himself up to standing.

He looked over triumphantly at Daniel.

"Clever," Daniel muttered. "All right. Let's go."

Noah's heart sank. Yes, he had stood up, but how the heck was he supposed to ski with this thing weighing him down?

It wasn't easy. Noah spent hours that day riding up the T-bar, only to fall trying to parallel ski with eighty pounds on his back. By mid-afternoon, welts had formed on his shoulders that split open and bled by evening. Snow began to come down, blurring Noah's vision and making it twice as hard to see.

Still, Daniel didn't let up.

Over and over again, he made Noah ride up the mountain and ski back down. All the progress Noah had made the day before slipped away with the extra weight on his back. Noah just wanted to sit down in the snow and quit, but with Daniel's keen eye on him every time he fell, he gritted his teeth, hoisted the bag back up, and tried again.

The snow stopped falling and the moon rose, light spilling in soft folds across the mountain. Somewhere in the distance, a lone wolf howled. Still, there was no letup.

"It's getting dark," Noah pointed out.

Daniel nodded. "So it is."

"Shouldn't we be heading back?" Noah suggested.

"Not until you master this," Daniel told him.

"I can try again tomorrow," Noah said, trying to keep the pleading from his voice. He was exhausted.

Daniel shook his head. "There is no tomorrow in war. There is only the moment. I know you don't like me much, Garrett, and that's fine. But I want you to understand that I wouldn't push you any harder than I push myself. Now go back up and ski down again."

Noah's mind grew numb. He couldn't feel his fingers or his cheeks. He didn't think about anything. He just skied up and down, up and down, until Daniel's voice was all he heard.

And then, suddenly, he did it. He skied the entire way down and didn't fall or stumble. He skied an almost perfect parallel. He came to a dead stop right in front of Daniel Stultz, spraying him with a shower of snow from his turning skis. The sight of the snow dusting Daniel's immaculate uniform gave Noah a great deal of satisfaction. He waited for Daniel's praise.

"You'll have to move faster than that to evade the Germans," Daniel said.

Noah closed his eyes. Was this man never satisfied?

"Still," Daniel continued, "you did all right today, considering you're not a natural athlete."

"Who said I'm not much of an athlete?" Noah snapped.

Daniel sighed. "Don't get so bent out of shape, Garrett. I just told you the truth, that's all. I believe in always being truthful. And I didn't say you weren't much of an athlete. I said you weren't a natural. Not everyone's a natural."

"Fine," Noah said, throwing down his poles. "Maybe I'm not a natural. I didn't grow up skiing. I grew up in Texas. But I worked hard on my farm, really hard."

Daniel shrugged. "Working hard on a farm and being a

natural athlete are two different things. What do you care anyway? Your whole attitude reeks of not wanting any of this, and I hate training anyone who doesn't truly believe in fighting this war. So, why *are* you here, Garrett?"

"I didn't have a choice," Noah shot back. "My parents died. My uncle is my only living relative. So unlike you, signing up was not my choice. When things get tough, at least you've got someone to write home and whine about it to. I'm all alone."

Daniel's eyes hardened. "What do you want? Sympathy from me? I haven't got any for you."

"No surprise there," Noah snapped. "I'm not sure you've got any feelings at all."

Daniel bent over to pick up Noah's poles. "We're done, Garrett. But I'll give you one last piece of advice, and for free, too."

His brown eyes bored into Noah's as he handed him his poles. "Assumptions can get you killed."

Then he turned his back on Noah and skied away, back toward the camp.

"I'M NOT GOING TO WAR, ANYWAY!" Noah wanted to shout after him, but he knew those words just might land his uncle in hot water. And even though Noah wanted to thrash his uncle for sticking him with Daniel Stultz these past two days, he knew he needed James Shelley — at least until he worked out a way to leave this camp for good.

Still, Noah felt relief. He was done with Daniel Stultz. The worst was over.

CHAPTER FOURTEEN

The mess hall was noisy that night, filled with boys who had sweated out another day of training in the mountains. The aroma of food and body odor mingled with the humidity of pants and boots drying after a day in knee-deep snow. Noah found a place next to his uncle and set his tray down.

"So, you've learned to ski," his uncle said, as he swiped a glob of gravy up with a piece of bread. "Somewhat, anyway."

"Daniel Stultz tell you that?" Noah asked, hating the "somewhat" he was sure Daniel had added.

His uncle shook his head. "Didn't have to. I was watching you at the end."

Noah felt himself redden.

"Not bad, boy," his uncle said, tossing the gravy-soaked bread into his mouth, "not bad at all for three days." He chewed the food and swallowed. "Looks like you inherited some skiing skills somewhere along the line."

At least his *uncle* had complimented his abilities. "Do you think my mother would have been a good skier?" Noah asked, wondering if his mother would have ever tried the sport had she lived a little longer.

His uncle was quiet for a moment. "I think your mother would have been good at anything she undertook, Noah."

Noah looked at James Shelley, but his uncle's face remained bland.

Roger tossed a tray of food down and slid onto the bench across from Noah and his uncle. "Okay. Let's hear it."

"Hear what?" Noah asked.

Wiley, Cam, and Bill came sidling up and sat down.

"Come on, Shelley," Roger said. "Let's hear the story."

"What story?" James Shelley asked, looking at the boys with wide-eyed innocence, but Noah could see the beginnings of a smile on his lips.

"The one Skeeter keeps telling everybody to ask you about," Roger said impatiently. "Something funny, he says. Come on. Tell us all what happened."

And as he had the night Noah arrived, Roger began to chant, "Tell it! Tell it! Tell it!" Soon the whole mess hall had joined in, pleading to hear the funny thing that had happened on the mountain. Somebody poked Noah in the ribs, and Noah joined in with the crowd.

James Shelley finally shook his head. "All right. All right. I'll tell it."

A sigh could have been heard in the room then, as the entire camp leaned forward expectantly.

"Well," Noah's uncle began, "I was out all day yesterday, experimenting with some new wool blankets Uncle Sam sent us that they think may hold up better under the unique conditions we find ourselves in when skiing at altitudes such as we do and with the temperatures dropping as we know they do at night around here and —"

"Get on with it, Shelley," Roger interrupted.

James Shelley grinned. "Patience, boy, patience."

Someone sent a Ping-Pong ball soaring into the air, landing it on the table with a loud *thwap*. "Patience is for Germans!"

"Okay," Noah's uncle laughed, holding his hands up in mock resignation. "Okay. I'll get to the good part.

"So, anyway," James Shelley continued, leaning forward, as if to tell a secret, though his voice grew loud enough to carry clearly across the large room. "I'm up on Homestake Peak, skiing the ridge. It's about ten below, and my hands and feet are numb, but I don't care. It's beautiful up there."

The boys nodded. Even Noah could imagine how it might look, high on the mountains that surrounded them, looking down upon the world in all its glory, the whitewashed camp buildings gleaming in all that snow and light.

"Then suddenly, over my two-way radio," his uncle continued, "I hear this pilot flying somewhere in the distance and sending back a signal to his base. And he's shouting, 'I'm at eight thousand feet and gliding, gliding!'"

James Shelley grinned. "I couldn't resist. I get on my radio and send this message back: 'And I'm at twelve thousand feet and walking, walking!'"

His uncle let out a loud guffaw, and the rest of the mess hall joined in. Noah burst out laughing, too. He could just imagine that pilot's surprise at hearing that someone was walking at an altitude higher than his.

Outside the mess hall, there was the sound of a jeep shifting gears and screeching to a halt.

A short while later, Skeeter came into the mess hall. "Shelley, someone's here to see you."

A woman barged in behind Skeeter, tottering on high-heeled shoes, her heavy winter coat just covering a flimsy skirt. Her cheeks, flushed from the cold, matched her heavily painted red lips. Several of the boys whistled.

"Hey, I told you to wait in the car! You're not allowed in here," Skeeter said, as he reached out and tried unsuccessfully to grab the woman, who ignored him and marched farther into the hall.

"Dana, darling!" Noah's uncle said, standing.

"Don't give me none of your sweet talk now, James Shelley," admonished the woman. "You leave me in Denver on a corner and say you'll be back, and then you don't show up ever. And I don't hear from you for weeks and weeks until you need —"

By this time, Noah's uncle had reached Dana, and he quickly slapped his hand over her mouth. The boys in the mess tent were roaring with laughter.

"Dana, honey," James Shelley said, "why don't we just go on outside and talk about this?"

He took her by the elbow and started steering her to the door. His hand was still over her mouth when suddenly he let out a yelp and jumped back from her, shaking a palm that was now red with teeth marks and lipstick.

"Shelley," the woman began again, "I ain't your woman after that night, so don't go getting your hopes up or anything. I'm only here 'cause Skeeter told me about —"

That was the last any of them heard. Skeeter had come up behind Dana and whisked her out the door.

"Hey, boys," James Shelley said, turning once before disappearing after Skeeter and the woman, "don't wait up for me tonight."

He winked, and the boys all cheered and clapped.

Noah pushed his food away and stared down at the table. He had just started to kind of like his uncle, with his jokes and his love of skiing and even the rough way he had about him. He had just started to see him as family. Now this woman had turned up, reminding Noah just what kind of man his uncle really was, probably why his parents had never acknowledged James Shelley's existence.

Noah stood.

"Where you going, Noah?" Wiley called after him, as Noah emptied his tray.

Noah didn't answer. He made his way outside, shrugging on his heavy coat. The night was cloudy and dark. A wind had picked up, probably meaning there would be snow again tomorrow. He looked at the mountains, rising dark against the horizon. Tonight, they seemed forbidding.

Noah's footsteps sounded hollow and lonely in the night air as he crunched along in the snow. He walked without thinking, listening to the wind, and, from somewhere behind him, radio music and laughter from the mess hall.

As he approached the end of the line of barracks, a soft braying floated through the air. Noah turned toward the sound, locating a building from which emanated the rustle of hooves and the smell of hay. He slid the doors of the barn open.

Noah had to strain to see as he made his way into the near-darkness. He stopped by the first stall and peered inside. There was the soft plod of mule feet and then a wet nose was exploring Noah's outstretched hands. Noah rubbed the soft coat of the mule and breathed in the animal's scent, a reminder of home and his old life.

A light flared within the dark of the barn. Noah jumped back, startled. Daniel Stultz stood there, cupping a match in his hand. He brought the flame to a cigarette in his mouth. There was a soft sizzle, and the scent of smoke filled the air. Daniel shook the match out and took a deep puff, flicking on a flashlight that was hanging from his belt as he did so and lighting up the corner of the barn in which they stood.

"Didn't know you were an animal lover, Garrett," Daniel said shortly, exhaling smoke from his mouth.

"I told you," Noah said, annoyed that this man, like a bad penny, had suddenly turned up once again, "I grew up on a farm."

"So, you're a mule expert?" Daniel asked.

"And you're a skiing expert," Noah shot back. "So what? What brings *you* here? Please don't tell me that *you're* some kind of animal lover!"

Daniel took another puff of his cigarette. "Hardly. But this old barn seems to be the only place to get a little peace and quiet around here." He looked Noah up and down. "But even that's ruined now." He inhaled one more time, then dropped the cigarette to the floor and stepped on it until the ember went out. "Good night, Garrett."

He turned and walked away.

Noah bent down to pick up the remnants of the cigarette and match, knowing that fire was one of the most feared dangers in a barn, but as he did so, he saw something hanging from the back of Daniel Stultz's pants pocket that gave him pause.

In the retreating light of Daniel's flashlight, Noah could just make out slender orange stalks and leafy green tops peeking out from Daniel's pockets. Daniel Stultz had brought more than a desire for peace and quiet to the barn. He'd brought a mule's favorite snack — carrots!

CHAPTER FIFTEEN

The next morning, Noah's uncle shook him awake.

"Where were you last night, boy?" he asked. "I looked high and low for you."

Noah rolled over. He'd fallen asleep in the barn, surrounded by the warmth of the mules and the soft pawing of hooves. He'd woken in the middle of the night and stumbled back to the barracks to find his uncle snoring loudly enough to cause an avalanche. There was no sign of the woman, Dana, anywhere.

"Seemed like you were busy," Noah said curtly.

The boys in the barracks all laughed. James Shelley flushed, and Noah was glad to have embarrassed him somewhat.

"What do you think this is? A vacation?" his uncle barked. "Get up. Olaf will be here any minute to take you out today."

Noah went to the showers and found Wiley there, already finished and almost dressed.

"Hey," Wiley said. "Where were you last night?"

Was everyone going to ask him the same thing?

"I just went for a walk," Noah said. "I needed some fresh air."

"Must have been a long walk," Wiley joked.

Noah didn't answer. He stripped and turned the water on.

"Hey," Wiley said, coming toward him, "you okay?"

Noah stepped into the shower, wincing as the water hit the welts on his shoulders he'd gotten skiing with Daniel. "Yeah. It was just a long day yesterday."

"But you're done, right?" Wiley said. "Dour Dan is back on maneuvers from what I hear."

Noah nodded. "Yeah, I'm out with someone named Olaf today."

Wiley grinned as he threw on a ski jacket and brushed back his hair. "Great! Now, you're on to the important part."

"The important part?" Noah called after him as Wiley headed for the door.

"Yeah." Wiley stopped and turned. "Olaf conducts combat training. In a few weeks, you'll be ready to go out with us big boys and won't that be some fun, eh, Noah?"

Noah's heart sank at Wiley's words. His uncle was sending him out today to train for combat?

"See you at dinner, soldier," Wiley called as he headed out into the cold.

Olaf was Norwegian, short and blond with piercing blue eyes and a heavy accent. He didn't hurry Noah while he packed his rucksack nor when it took Noah several attempts to attach seal-skins to his skis in anticipation of what Olaf called "our little climb." But once Noah was outfitted, Olaf had him skiing out of camp at breakneck speed.

An hour into the hike up the mountain, Noah was weak with fatigue. Snow had started to fall, coming down so fast and hard, Noah could barely see in front of him. The pack on his back felt as if it weighed three hundred pounds, not eighty. Already, Noah could feel the welts from yesterday beginning to reopen. He shifted his shoulders to settle the rucksack on less sore skin, but it didn't help. And just as it had when Noah first arrived, the air itself was making it difficult to breathe.

At last, they came to a kind of camp, high in the hills, with military tanks, shooting ranges, and tents. Olaf came to a halt, and Noah skied up beside him, wearily letting his rucksack fall to the ground.

The snow had stopped. Olaf took off his skis and walked over to a large equipment building. He unlocked a padlock and disappeared inside, returning in a few minutes with a gun.

"Can you shoot?" he asked.

Noah looked at the rifle. He had used a similar one in Texas. "Yes, I used to hunt with my dad."

"Follow along, then. Take off your skis and come vith me," Olaf said, walking toward the shooting range.

When they were several hundred feet from the targets, Olaf stopped. "Let us see vhat you can do."

Noah took the gun from Olaf. He raised the gun to his shoulder, aimed at the red center of the target, and pulled the trigger. Nothing happened.

Olaf's laughter rang out in the quiet of that snow-covered mountain camp. "Perhaps it vould be best if you vould check for ammunition first?" He took a box of bullets from the pocket of his ski parka and grinned wickedly at Noah.

Noah snatched up the bullets and loaded eight of them into the gun, shoving each one into the chamber until he heard it make a satisfying click.

"Oh, the boys vill have a good laugh over this tonight." Olaf chuckled, as Noah raised the rifle to his shoulder again.

Noah felt his face grow hot. First Daniel Stultz and now this!

Concentrating carefully on the target, Noah squinted down the barrel. He shot off five rounds, hitting the bull's-eye every time. Then he turned toward Olaf, swinging the gun with him until he was looking down the shaft at a spot very near Olaf himself. The threat he posed was unmistakable.

"Were you saying something before I shot?" Noah asked, his tone sharp and bitter.

Olaf didn't flinch. Taking two fingers and lightly turning the barrel of the rifle back toward the target, he grinned at Noah. "I vas just saying that it vas too bad that the boys vill hear *nothing* about this little incident, eh?"

Noah relaxed. Then, to be sure Olaf would keep his silence, he turned quickly and shot off three more rounds, emptying the rifle directly into the center of the target.

"And so you can shoot," Olaf said, as Noah lowered the rifle and looked at him.

"And so I can shoot," Noah agreed.

From now on, anyone who trained him would understand that Noah wasn't to be fooled around with. He'd show them just how tough he could be. Round one of *this* contest was his.

"The gun is yours now," Olaf said, taking the rifle from Noah, walking back to Noah's rucksack, and tying the rifle to it. "And ve can move on to the next part of your training."

He handed Noah his skis and poles again, picking up his own in the process. "You must now learn to crawl along the ground vhen the shots are being fired above your head. You must learn to pull your skis and poles along vith you, as you vill need them vhen you reach your destination. Vatch now."

Olaf marched to an empty field with barbed wire in the center of the flat area. He dropped to the ground, tying his skis and poles close to his side with some rope. Then he began to use his elbows to crawl, keeping his head low and his skiing equipment sliding along beside him. When he reached the barbed wire, he lifted it as carefully as possible and scooted beneath it, the poles and skis moving along with him until he disappeared into a ditch on the other side. Finally, he stood.

"Any questions?" he called out to Noah.

Noah shook his head. Questions? What wouldn't he understand? This was easy.

Olaf walked back toward Noah and motioned him toward the field.

"Your turn, then," he said, sitting down.

Noah took his skis and poles and walked out into the open field. He dropped to the ground in the wet snow at the same point where Olaf had begun the exercise and tied his skis and poles to his waist. Slowly, he began crawling toward the barbed wire. Suddenly, shots rang out over his head. Noah jerked around to look behind him when another shot whizzed past his ear. Olaf was pointing a gun toward Noah's head! Noah watched as Olaf yawned and then fired a few more rounds over Noah.

"What are you trying to do?" Noah cried out. "Kill me?"

The firing stopped. Olaf grinned. "No, *I* vill not kill you, but the *Germans* may if you don't crawl a little faster." He fired again.

That was all Noah needed. As quickly as he could, he scooted toward the barbed wire and pulled himself and his skis and poles under it until he was safely in the ditch on the other side. His heart was racing, and his breath came in quick, frozen gulps. The man was crazy! They were all crazy!

"Come out now." Olaf's voice floated across the snow.

Noah hesitated. What if Olaf shot at him when he stood up?

"Noah!" Olaf barked for the first time that day. "I have vaited for you patiently, but ve do not have all day. Stand up now!"

Uneasily, Noah rose from the ditch.

Olaf grinned. "All right then, my little shooter. Let us try again. But perhaps this time, you vill move a little *quicker*, no?" He threw back his head and laughed, the sound echoing across the empty field.

Noah scowled. The insane Norwegian had just won round two!

CHAPTER SIXTEEN

For the rest of the day, Noah crawled along the wet, snowy ground, pulling his skis beside him, praying that the bullets zinging past his head wouldn't hit him. They stopped only once, for a quick bite of lunch, and then Olaf commanded Noah to begin again. Finally, the light began to fade a little, and Olaf stood up. He stretched and yawned. "That is it for the day. Ve should head back now to be sure ve get to camp before the light has gone."

Noah picked up his rucksack and prepared to ski home. Already, he could feel his shoulders bleeding from the workout he'd had yesterday, but now they were also shaky from crawling about on his elbows for hours across that field.

The addition of the rifle didn't help. The pack wasn't any heavier, at least not in any way that Noah could determine, but the gun was unwieldy, jutting out in a vertical line from the rucksack. Three times, Noah was tripped up by it as he skied down the mountain, and not once did Olaf help him up.

"Am I doing something wrong?" Noah cried out in frustration the second time he landed headfirst in the snow. He'd come up with a mouthful of icy crystals and a cramp in his leg.

Olaf shrugged. "It is just something you vill have to get used to, Noah. The rifle makes it awkward. But you must carry it there. If you move it somevhere else, you vill not be able to reach it should you need it quickly. You vill always have to think about it a little as you ski. Even I have to remember it is there, and ski so that it does not get in the vay. And you must especially remember it vhen ve are at var. You must know vhere your rifle is and ski so that it does not interfere vith your moving about."

War was the one instance Noah knew he *wouldn't* have to remember the stupid rifle. He wasn't going. Ever!

At the bottom of the mountain, Olaf gave him a nod. "Tomorrow, then." He skied off. Wearily, Noah skied back to his barracks and opened the door to a welcome bit of warmth.

"You look done in," Noah's uncle said.

"Olaf put you through your paces, eh?" Wiley asked, grinning.

"He shot at me!" Noah said indignantly.

Wiley burst out laughing. "At least he only shot *at* you. Roger over there truly did get shot!"

Noah stared in disbelief as Roger pulled down the neck of his shirt to show him a scar on the top part of his arm.

"How can Olaf do that and get away with it?" Noah cried.

"We're training for war, Noah," James Shelley said. "This is not a game. This is serious business. It's important that you follow the rules. Not doing as your commander tells you can get you killed when you go into battle. Roger's lucky Olaf has such good reflexes. Otherwise he'd have lost his head and not just been hit in the arm! If it had been the Germans, Roger would have been dead."

"But Olaf wounded his own man!" Noah protested.

"Roger shouldn't have gotten up," James Shelley responded tersely.

Roger grinned. "Yeah, I won't be doing that again anytime soon when there's shots going off around me. Hurt like the blazes, and I don't mean to repeat the experience."

"And that's exactly what an officer wants to hear his men say," James Shelley agreed. "In war, there isn't time to argue. You've got to do as you're told and not think about it."

"Thinking on your own can get you in trouble," Bill offered. "In war, it's a team effort, Noah."

Noah looked at them in shock. They seemed to think it was perfectly all right to be shot by your commanding officer! Did the men in charge in Washington realize the insanity of this group? What if these crazies were sent to war? For once, Noah was truly aware that these boys were nothing but a bunch of insane skiers. They'd never be called into action. They'd never be sent overseas. The pilots on that train to Denver had been right, and Noah was grateful for it. Only an idiot would send these men to war.

The next morning, Noah was back at the mountain camp. Olaf handed him a shovel.

"Today," he said, "ve vill dig the foxhole, no? It is good to have the deep foxhole vhen the rifle is being fired above your head."

Noah took the shovel and followed Olaf to a spot several feet away.

"Dig," Olaf commanded.

Noah struck the snowy ground with the shovel. It was rock hard. He struck over and over. Olaf went and sat in the snow again. Noah watched him uneasily. Would he shoot at him as he dug?

Olaf lit up a cigarette and gazed off at the mountains. Relaxing a bit, Noah went back to digging. It was impossible. The ground was almost solid. Noah managed only a small chunk of dirt with each dig of the shovel. His shoulders began to ache again, and his body shook with the tension of hitting frozen ground.

An hour went by. And then another. The hole was still tiny. As time passed, Noah grew more exhausted and angrier. He felt like throwing down the shovel. Why was he spending his day like this? What was he doing? He was *never* going to war. He *wouldn't*. There was *nothing* that could *ever* make him go! His uncle knew he was underage. All this practicing for war was a waste of his time — and Olaf's! He would tell his uncle this tonight.

The sun began to drop, and the temperature with it. Noah kept on digging. Finally, he had a hole large enough that he could fit down inside.

He stood up, groaning with pain. "It's done."

Olaf looked at the hole. "*Ja*, but can you hide in it? Vill it protect you?"

"Sure," Noah said, "good enough. I mean, how deep am I supposed to build one of these things with the ground so hard?"

"Get into the hole," Olaf commanded.

Noah did as Olaf said, curling up in a ball so Olaf could see how well he fit into the hole he had dug. Noah waited. Olaf would probably shoot a few rounds over his head, and he would see that the hole was big enough for Noah to avoid getting hit.

Then Noah heard the sound of a motor starting up. The ground gave a groan and then a rumble. What the heck?

He raised his head just in time to see a huge tank coming his way. Noah turned to look behind him. There was nowhere to run quickly enough to get out of the way. Noah ducked down into his hole, making himself as small as possible.

With a roar and groan, the tank sped over the foxhole, stopping just a few yards beyond. Noah waited. The sound of the engine died away. Cautiously, Noah raised himself up.

Olaf was standing in the hatch of the tank.

"What was that for?" Noah shouted in anger.

"The Germans," Olaf said, "they do not care if they hurt or kill you. In fact, that is vhat they vant. So you dig a deep foxhole. You have made one that is sufficient. You vould have survived."

Noah stared at Olaf, trembling from anger and the fright of the big tank passing over him. He watched Olaf casually light up another cigarette and stare off into space again.

They're nuts. They're all *nuts,* he thought. He would never see a German or a Japanese in his life. He wasn't going into battle. He couldn't kill anyone. Just like his parents, he didn't believe in it. All this stomping around in the snow was craziness. He was getting out of here, today, tomorrow, as soon as he could.

Then Noah remembered his uncle's conversation with Skeeter. He felt a sudden shiver down his spine. What if he couldn't make arrangements fast enough? Even if their special skills would prove useless in the Pacific or Africa, with more men being lost every day, the army had every right to deploy the Phantoms anywhere, at any time, and use them in any way they saw fit. If military officials in Washington suddenly called the Phantoms into action, would James Shelley be crazy enough to make Noah go with him? And since they had all lied, Noah to his uncle, his uncle to the general, would the general think he was really sixteen and send him? Noah had to get himself out of this situation. And fast.

CHAPTER SEVENTEEN

That night in the mess hall, Noah decided again to approach his uncle about leaving. "Uncle Shelley, can I talk to you?"

"Sure," his uncle said, moving over to make room for Noah next to him.

"Alone," Noah added.

His uncle's eyebrows shot up. But he stood, and Noah followed him outside. A supply truck had arrived, and boys were unloading food into the kitchen attached to the mess hall. Noah led his uncle away from the noise and confusion until they were standing at the edge of the camp. There, Noah halted.

"I . . . ," he began, then stopped. Should he tell his uncle he had heard the conversation with Skeeter? Should he admit to lying and talk to his uncle about alternative possibilities? His uncle had said he didn't want to send him to an orphanage. Perhaps together they could come up with another plan.

"I . . . ," Noah began again.

"Spit it out, boy," Noah's uncle said, running his hand through hair that had not been washed in several days. "It's cold enough out here to freeze a polar bear, and I got to plan some maneuvers for tomorrow."

"This isn't going so well for me," Noah started tentatively.

James Shelley threw back his head and laughed. "Ain't that what every new recruit says? If I had a nickel for every time I've heard that line, I'd be a wealthy man there, Noah boy."

"I'm not a recruit," Noah argued. "I'm not even —"

"Well, you are now," Noah's uncle assured him. "I just turned the paperwork over to the general. You're all signed up. Good as gold, boy. Good as gold. No orphanage for you. You've got a home now and family to look after you."

James Shelley beamed with satisfaction. "This little problem of you showing up is all solved for the time being. You're a regular member of the 86th, Noah. Proud and strong we are. Proud and strong."

He was all signed up? How was that possible? He wasn't old enough to sign up!

"How?" Noah began.

"You leave the how to me," his uncle told him.

"But I don't *believe* in war!" Noah cried out in horror.

James Shelley let out a loud guffaw, shocking Noah. "Who the heck does, boy?"

"Everybody here," Noah said, sweeping his hand across the camp. "You all believe in fighting and guns and all those other things."

Noah's uncle shook his head. "You got that all wrong, Noah.

Nobody here *believes* in war. Nobody here *wants* war. But that's what we got anyhow. Now just stop your fussing and listen up a minute."

His uncle's eyes were suddenly serious and hard as ice. "You're safe here. You've got a home. You got a roof over your head and food to eat. In a country that's just beginning to recover from an economic crisis of massive proportions, I'd say that ain't bad. Yeah, I know it's a bit rough, the training. And I know you're a bit lonely, with your parents gone and all that. I get it. But you're starting to make some friends now — Wiley, Roger, Cam, and Bill. And you've got me watching your back. Seems to me, most orphans might even be grateful for what you got. Ain't you grateful, Noah?"

Noah stared miserably at his uncle. What could he say? That was certainly one of the most heartfelt speeches he'd ever heard his uncle make. And put that way, Noah had to admit, it sounded as if he was whining. And Noah knew his uncle *hated* whiny people.

"Of course I'm grateful, Uncle Shelley," Noah said. "I didn't mean to sound as if I wasn't."

"'Course not," his uncle said. "I know that."

James Shelley swung his arm over Noah's shoulders. "Now let's go get us some chow, boy. You got to keep your strength up for training, eh?"

Noah let his uncle lead him back to the mess hall. His uncle would be no help. Noah would just have to hope that a letter arrived from Reverend Patterson and that he would somehow get Noah out of this mess.

Seven weeks passed. Every day, Noah worked on his skiing ability, growing better and better. He began to like the feel of flying down the slope, controlling his turns, going as fast as he could. He continued training with Olaf, digging foxholes and shooting. He returned to the barracks at night, sweaty and exhausted, but there was a strange satisfaction in the hard physical work. He could feel his strength building the harder he pushed himself.

Still, every day Noah went to the Army Post Office, hoping to have a letter from Reverend Patterson.

One day, Olaf led him in a different direction from the mountain training camp.

"Where are we going?" Noah shouted up to him as they skied away from Camp Hale.

"You vill see," Olaf called back.

Noah followed him until they stood at the top of a high cliff.

"Skis off," Olaf ordered.

Noah did as Olaf told him.

"And so today, ve learn how to rappel down a mountain," Olaf said, taking a rope and wrapping it around a boulder.

"I'm going down *that*?" Noah exclaimed, looking over at the great drop below him and at the thinness of the rope. "Using just *that*?"

"*Ja*," Olaf said. He turned and tied the rope to a metal ring that was attached to a stake that had been driven into the rock.

"Why?" Noah asked. "It's not as if there are going to be these metal rings on top of mountains in the middle of a war."

Olaf laughed. "Of course not. Vhen you have to go down the side of an untried mountain, vhether to escape or to attack, *you* vill have to drive the piton in first yourself and attach the carabiner before you go."

"How in the heck do I do that?" Noah asked, fear in his throat at the idea of trusting some small metal stake and ring he had just driven into hard rock without someone testing it first.

"Next time, I vill teach you," Olaf said. "For today, ve just rappel down."

Olaf looped the doubled rope between his legs, around one thigh and over his body and up past his neck to his hands. Then, in horror, Noah watched Olaf lean way out, until only the soles of his boots were touching the mountainside.

"Vee hoo!" Olaf shouted, grinning. And with a giant leap, he let the rope slide through his hands, bouncing his way down the mountainside, swinging out and then in, where his boots kicked against the rock of the mountain before he slid several more feet down.

Noah could barely breathe just watching him.

Olaf reached the base of the mountain. "Your turn, Noah," he called up. "The rope you should use is lying next to you."

Noah wondered if he could just pretend not to find it. Then when Olaf came back up to help him search, he could toss it over the side when Olaf wasn't looking. But what was the point? He'd just be putting it off for another day. There would always be more rope back at the camp. He would have to do this sometime.

Noah picked up the line. It was made of a strange material he had never felt before. He stood with the two ends, trying to remember how Olaf had done it. He tugged on the rope, and it gave a little.

"Are you sure this is strong enough to hold me?" he called down. "You know you're much smaller than I am."

Olaf laughed. "This rope is very strong, Noah. It does not fray. The material is new and is called nylon, and it is very good. You vill be fine. Now tie the rope like this."

Below him, Olaf demonstrated how to secure himself with the rope, and Noah followed his example.

"Now lean back, and plant your feet against the side of the mountain," Olaf ordered.

Noah took a deep breath. This was it. He was petrified. He leaned back, fighting the instinct to scramble to safety at the top of the mountain. Below him, the world seemed a great distance away. His head played out the image of himself free-falling to the bottom. He thought he was going to throw up.

"Now bounce a bit," Olaf called, "and let the rope slip through your hands."

Inside his gloves, Noah's hands were sweating. He steadied himself, said a quick prayer under his breath, and bounced back, doing as Olaf instructed. Immediately, he fell several feet, his breath coming out of him in a great big gasp. He gripped the rope again and stopped, banging hard against the mountainside.

"Good," Olaf yelled up. "But keep going. In a var, you vill not be able to stop every few feet, Noah. You vill need to be quick."

Noah sighed. It was always about speed: speed in skiing, speed in shooting, speed in crawling, and speed in rappelling down a mountainside. He wished he could speed up the fear, too, and get to the calm faster.

"Come on now, Noah," Olaf commanded.

Noah looked down at the ground below. He felt dizzy. He took a deep breath again and let the rope slide. This time, when his boots hit the mountain, he didn't let himself stop. Instead, he pushed hard against the rock, and let himself slide down even farther. Fear rose in his throat as he flew toward the mountainside again. He forced himself to forget the fear and to just keep going. When Noah reached the bottom, he looked up to where he had started and pride at his courage rushed over him.

"Good job," Olaf said. "Now, let's do it again."

They hiked back up. This time around, Noah just let himself fly, and soon found himself in a rhythm. In, push, fly out, loosen your grip, slide down, over and over. It was like being an eagle or a kite sliding down that mountain so smoothly, the world at your feet and you coming toward it as fast as you could manage. When you just let yourself go, it was an amazing feeling!

Again and again they practiced, until on their final run, Noah and Olaf shouted with joy as together they propelled down. Noah loved doing this! And Olaf, too, seemed pleased.

When they got back to camp, Noah was on a high, in spite of the shaking of his arms from the effort of that afternoon. On his way back to the barracks, he stopped to check for mail, and found to his surprise that there was a letter for him. Noah's heart skipped a beat. The return address was Reverend Patterson's. He sat down and ripped the letter open.

Dear Noah:

Son, I was glad to get your letter and to hear that your uncle has provided for you in your time of loss. I wish I could be more encouraging about you coming home and finding work. I know your folks were opposed to war, Noah, but I've spent some time asking around and there isn't anything here. At least there, you have food and shelter. You are too young to be shipped out just yet and so this seems the only avenue available right now. I will keep my eyes and ears open for other possibilities, but the community is hard up. Another mouth to feed is something that most folks around here cannot afford.

May God keep you, my son.
Reverend Patterson

Noah closed the letter and stared down at the floor.

Just then, Wiley plopped down beside him. "Hey, Noah. We got a day off tomorrow. Me and the boys are going into Leadville. You want to come?"

"What's in Leadville?" Noah asked dispiritedly.

Wiley leaned in close. "A little bit of wild."

Noah turned to look at Wiley. His red hair was sticking out in all directions, and a wicked grin lit up his face.

"Wiley," Noah said, ripping Reverend Patterson's letter in two, "count me in."

A little bit of wild? Noah Garrett needed just that right about now.

CHAPTER EIGHTEEN

Noah's uncle frowned when he heard of Noah's plans to go to Leadville. "Be better if you rested, let those muscles of yours loosen up during your day off."

"Aw, come on, Shelley," Roger said. "The kid needs a break. We're just going for dinner and overnight. Where's the harm?"

"The harm is in my nephew going along with you *bozos*," James Shelley said.

"Hey," Bill argued, "he's of age. He can handle himself."

"Yeah," Noah said. "I'm of age."

Noah's uncle shot him a look, then nodded. "All right, but I'm expecting you to take care of him."

"Yes, sir," Wiley said, popping to attention and saluting Shelley.

"Yeah, yeah," James Shelley said, waving Wiley off. "Get out of here."

Noah followed Wiley, Roger, Bill, and Cam out the door, a duffel bag with clothes for overnight in his hand.

"Man, your uncle sure doesn't give you much credit. I mean you signed up for *war*, for Pete's sake. He acts like you're a kid or something," Cam complained as they picked up their skis and poles.

Cam had no idea just how true that statement was. Noah shrugged. "Family. What can you say?"

Wiley laughed. "Ain't that the truth?"

They all jumped into a jeep, throwing their bags, skis, and poles in the back. Soon they were roaring down a snow-covered road, sashaying back and forth fast enough to make most people sick. But the boys of the 86th laughed as they careened from side to side, and Noah joined in. Cam, Roger, and Wiley began teasing Bill, who was trying to read a letter from his sweetheart back home.

"What's her name?" Noah asked.

"Suzie," Bill replied.

"Ooooh, Suzie," Roger crooned. "Marry me, Suzie."

"Oh, shut up," Bill said, punching Roger, who was driving. "With that ugly mug of yours, you'll never even get a girl. Heck, it's lucky they even let you in the army."

Not too far from camp, the jeep abruptly came to a halt.

"What are we stopping for?" Noah asked as Wiley jumped out.

"You'll see," Roger said, grinning.

Wiley took a rope out of the jeep, went to the back of the vehicle, looped the rope around the bumper, and then put on his skis.

He took the rope in his hands and gave Roger a thumbs-up sign. Roger took off, the jeep fishtailing a bit, and Wiley, holding on for dear life, shouted with joy at the top of his lungs. Noah laughed, watching him.

They each took turns skiing behind the jeep as they sped toward Leadville. When Noah's turn came, he felt a flicker of fear, but he managed to hold on, even when the jeep went careening around an icy curve. At the end, Noah was sweating profusely, yet marveling at the thrill of the ride.

Cam was the last one to ski. Wiley, who was driving this time, floored the jeep and sped down the road. Cam was hooting and hollering, and they were all laughing as Cam tried to ski from side to side. They rounded a curve, and Cam's eyes suddenly widened. Noah turned to look. There was a mailbox on the side of the road. Cam couldn't move back to center fast enough. He smashed into the box, letting go of the towrope in the process. Wiley slammed on the brakes, sending the jeep into a ninety-degree turn before coming to a stop.

They all jumped out of the car and hurried back to the mailbox. Cam was sitting up and looking a bit woozy.

"Cam!" Wiley shouted. "Are you all right?"

"Didn't see that coming!" Cam slurred before falling over into a heap.

"Get him into the jeep," Roger commanded them.

As if they were in the midst of battle, the boys all went into action. Bill took one of Cam's legs and Wiley took the other. Roger grabbed Cam's right arm, and Noah took the left. They raced toward the jeep, Cam's dead weight throwing them from side to side. Carefully, they placed Cam in the back, and then, squishing into the front together, started the jeep up again and turned it around.

"Is there a hospital in Leadville?" Noah asked as they sped on.

"Don't know," Bill said, his face white. "We've never needed one before."

"What'll we do if he's hurt bad?" Wiley asked. His voice shook.

"We're idiots," Roger said angrily.

Noah couldn't agree with him more. He felt awful about this.

"This is all my fault," Wiley said, shaking his head. "I was driving."

"Cam's tough. He'll survive this."

"I sure hope so," Roger said, taking a curve. "The sound of him hitting that mailbox was awful."

"And he hit it hard."

"Yeah," Wiley said. "Even the jeep shuddered."

"But it will make a good story."

"A good story?" Noah sputtered. "How can anyone think about that at a time like this?"

"Seems as good a thing to think about as anything else."

Who was being so callous? They all looked at one another, and then finally turned to the backseat. Cam was sitting up, looking fine and grinning away. "I think I might even have your *uncle* beat with this story, Garrett!"

The laughter that filled the jeep was louder than before, filled mainly with relief.

| ▮ | ▮ |

Leadville was a little town of nothing. There were no shops or movie theaters, and the only restaurant in town was the one in the hotel. Still, it felt great to have a room with a real bath, heat, and a pillow and lots of blankets. The boys ate a big steak dinner, and then sat before the fire, talking late into the night.

"My parents are teachers," Bill said, "and when I come back from the war, I'm going to go to college to get a degree and then go home to teach. For me, there's no place on earth that can match Bonners Ferry, Idaho."

"Especially with Suzie by your side?" Wiley ribbed him.

"Sure," Bill said, turning red. "Wouldn't be a bad life, being married to her and teaching school. I've never had any desire to wander too far from home. Even being here in Colorado makes me homesick."

"Not the path for me," Roger said. "I don't intend to ever marry. I like freedom too much. I've seen my two sisters marry and have kids and work themselves to the bone. Heck, my father spent all his life in Vermont strapped to maple trees pulling syrup just to get by. I want no part of that. Give me the open road and a motorcycle, no responsibilities and a life of adventure."

"I don't know," Cam spoke up. "Wouldn't you miss seeing your family, Roger? I miss my mom and my dad and my little brother.

"He's only eight, you know," Cam said, turning to Noah. "You should have seen how proud he was of me when I left to join the war effort."

He pulled out a picture and showed Noah. Cam stood on the right with his hand draped around a little boy missing his two front teeth.

"I hope I live up to what he expects from me," Cam said. "I'd sure hate to come home without a medal or two to show him. I miss him like crazy."

"Aw, you just miss your mom's cooking," Wiley teased him.

Cam grinned. "Well, there's that, too."

"So, what about you, Noah?" Bill asked. "How'd you end up being one of us?"

Noah told them his own story, even opening up about his parents' death. By the end of the evening, Noah felt as if he had known these four all his life.

When Noah bunked down in the twin-bedded room he was sharing with Wiley, he was amazed at how warm and comfortable he was for the first time in a long time. He slept heavily.

Just before dawn, Wiley shook him awake.

"What?" he asked groggily, staring up at Wiley, who was fully dressed with his duffel bag beside him. "What's wrong?"

"Nothing," Wiley said. "Hurry up. Get dressed and packed."

Noah was so sleepy, he did as Wiley commanded without asking why. But as he put on his pants, he came fully awake.

"What are we doing?" he finally asked.

Wiley put a finger to his lips. "Shh, we don't want to wake the other guests. You ready for a little bit of wild?"

Noah stopped dressing. Hadn't yesterday's race to Leadville been wild enough?

"Me and the boys have been planning this for a long time now," Wiley said, grinning. "And since you've just finished your cliff training, we knew you were the man to include in this *experiment.*"

Wiley paused. "Last time we were here, Bill noticed how high the sides of the hotel are. We did a little reconnaissance work and then asked for rooms on the top floor."

Noah looked at Wiley, puzzled.

"We're going to rappel down the side of the hotel and then ski off before they can catch us!" Wiley crowed softly.

Noah stared at him. "What if we get caught?"

Wiley laughed. "Chicken, Garrett?"

Noah thought about it a minute. Was he chicken? So what if they got caught? What could they do to him? Kick him out of the 86th?

"Let's go," Noah said, swinging his duffel bag onto his shoulder and giving Wiley a grin and a nod.

The sun was just coming up over the horizon as the boys leaned out of their hotel windows and began their descent. Each was spaced just a few feet from the other. Their duffel bags were on their backs, along with their skis and poles. Noah was the first to push off, the thrill of rappelling and the thought of getting caught making his heart thump hard in his chest. He let the rope slip through his hands and silently slid down ten feet, coming up hard against the side of the hotel. He pushed off again, trying to quiet the laughter that was building inside him as he watched Roger, Bill, Cam, and Wiley bouncing down the wall near him. They looked like spiders, wending their way through the air, attached by thin strings of thread.

Two more bounces, and they were almost to the bottom. The sun's rays were reflecting off the snow. A bird began its early morning tune. The air was crisp and clear, and Noah was elated as he slid down the side of the hotel as fast as he could. He vaulted again and went flying out. Just a few feet from him, he watched as Cam swung toward the hotel and saw a look of horror cross Cam's face, followed by the sound of breaking glass. Cam had swung into one of the hotel's windows. A woman's scream echoed out into the quiet of the morning.

"Holy Moses!" Wiley shouted. "Let's get out of here!"

Noah didn't have to be prompted. With a speed he didn't even know he had, he swung down the last few feet. Hands shaking, he undid his skis and threw them to the ground.

"What the heck!" A man stuck his head out another window of the hotel, staring at Wiley, Bill, and Roger as they flew past. Cam was right behind them, and Noah breathed a sigh of relief that he had not been hurt when he hit the glass. At last, they were all down.

Another head popped out of the broken window above them. "Hey!" The hotel manager's face was tight with anger. "You boys get back here this instant!"

"Yeah, right," Roger muttered as he attached his ski boots to his skis. "To the woods, boys!" And they were off, skiing as fast as they could, putting as much distance as possible between themselves and the hotel.

Noah thought of nothing but skiing, making sure not to fall, pushing himself as hard as he could. Faster and faster they skied across fields and down hillsides. Until at last they stopped, breathing heavily, sweat dripping down their faces.

"Whoo ha!" Wiley crowed. "Now, that was some fun!"

"*This* will be a story for camp!" Bill laughed. "I couldn't believe it when your feet hit that window."

"*You* couldn't believe it?" Cam said, grimacing. "The woman standing there in her slip and curlers couldn't believe it, either."

"That's a sight I would like to have seen," Roger hooted.

"Nah, you wouldn't have," Cam said, rolling his eyes. "She was about seventy!"

They all burst out laughing. Only Noah wasn't joining in.

"Noah?" Wiley said. "You all right? Something the matter?"

Noah looked at them, a feeling coming over him as if someone were running fingernails down his spine. "What about the jeep?"

CHAPTER NINETEEN

"M an, we are in for it now," Cam said, shaking his head.

"Yeah, we've *got* to go and get that vehicle," Bill said.

"Shoot. Last year, me and a few friends from my football team bought some girls' panties and began to string them up on the rival team's yards," Roger said.

"And the point of this is?" Bill asked.

"Word got around fast. By the fifth house, they had people waiting for us," Roger said. "We may have to wait till sundown to sneak back and get that jeep. They may be watching for us."

"But we're due back on the base at nineteen hundred hours," Cam said. "If we wait till dark, we'll be cutting it close."

"We don't have a choice," Noah argued. "We can't return now. Roger's right. There's probably people out looking for us."

They all stared dejectedly at one another.

Wiley took off his duffel bag and threw it to the ground. Then he sat down. "Some day off."

"Yeah," Cam said, tossing his bag down, too, and throwing himself on top of it. "We don't even have anything to eat with us."

"You always just think of food, Cam," Bill said. "We could get court-martialed for this."

"Yeah," Roger said ruefully. "We're gonna be in big trouble, no doubt."

He paused and then a wide grin suddenly lit up his face. "Still, you have to admit it, boys, the climb down that hotel sure was sweet, wasn't it?"

At this, they all burst out laughing, and this time, even Noah joined in.

Eventually, they skied back toward town, miserably cold from sitting in the snow all day and worried about getting back to Camp Hale on time without getting caught. They left their skis by the side of the road about a mile away from town and walked toward Leadville, keeping themselves hidden in the trees that bordered the road.

The hotel was quiet. The sun had just set, and shadows were creeping across the parking lot. Noah and the boys breathed a sigh of relief when they saw the jeep in the exact same spot they had parked it yesterday.

"Okay. Here's our strategy," Roger whispered to them. "You boys wait here. I'll sneak on in and get it. If anyone comes out when I start her up, take off."

"No, Roger," Noah argued. "That isn't right. We're in this together. If one of us gets caught, we all get caught."

"I'm with Noah," Bill agreed. "We're a team. Teams don't leave members behind."

Wiley and Cam nodded their assent.

With their eyes peeled for any sign of movement, the boys crouched low and scurried toward the jeep. Noah reached the vehicle first, and, keeping a hand firmly on the door to keep it from making a noise, he pulled down on the handle and carefully eased the jeep door open.

A face in the front seat turned toward him.

"Forget something, did we, Garrett?" Daniel Stultz asked.

"How did you think we wouldn't hear about this?" James Shelley raged. "Are you all total fools?"

Noah stood at attention along with Bill, Cam, Roger, and Wiley. His uncle's face was bright red, and spittle was coming from his mouth. Noah could see he was shaking.

"The police called here! Here!" James Shelley yelled, as he paced the room. "They're not idiots in Leadville. Boys rappelling out of their hotel rooms can only mean one thing — the 86th! You've disgraced this unit!"

He whirled around. "You're all on latrine cleanup for three weeks. Now get out of here!"

Noah went to follow the others, who were racing for the door, but his uncle held him back. "Not you. You stay!"

His uncle was quiet for a moment after everyone had gone.

The stillness was almost worse than the shouting. Noah shifted his weight uneasily, just as his uncle turned to face him.

"The day I ran away from home, I went away for good, Noah," his uncle said. "I never intended to see or hear from my family again."

He paused, and Noah felt his chest constrict.

"Then you showed up, and I did what I thought best. I kept you. I didn't turn you out." His uncle shook his head. "Now, I know this ain't the best place for a kid. But it is a home of some sorts, and you're safe at least." He paused. "You've sorely disappointed me."

Noah felt as if he'd been punched in the stomach. He had never imagined he could feel so badly.

James Shelley looked right at Noah. "And I didn't even owe you a thing, boy."

Noah felt like a knife had gone through him at his uncle's words.

"Then you don't owe me a lecture on how to behave, either!" Noah muttered.

James Shelley sighed, and without another word, he turned and walked away, leaving Noah standing alone in the barracks.

"Daniel didn't need to report us!" Noah fumed to the others when they stood together outside the mess hall later that night. A feeling was building inside him that made him want to punch the very walls of the buildings around him.

"Maybe he was afraid someone would find out if he hushed it up," Bill said reasonably. "He does take this life pretty seriously."

"Who would have found out?" Noah raged. "He took the call himself. He could have just driven to Leadville without saying anything to anyone and smoothed it all over. But no, not Daniel Stultz. He sits in wait like some kind of animal and then pounces on us when we come back to get the jeep!"

"Perhaps you'd like to tell me that to my face," Daniel said as he stepped out of the mess hall.

Noah swung around. "I'd be happy to! Soldiers don't rat on other soldiers, Stultz! I've only been here for two months, and already even I know that!"

"This is a military base, Garrett," Daniel said. "Not a circus!"

"It was just one lousy prank, some harmless fun!" Noah shouted. "You have *heard* of the word, haven't you?"

"Noah, forget it," Wiley said, trying to hold him back. "This isn't worth it."

Angrily, Noah shook him off. He was sick of Daniel Stultz. He was furious with his uncle for saying that he didn't owe Noah anything. He was sick of feeling alone and lonely and out of place. He was sick of everything!

"Have you even *heard* of the word?" Noah taunted Daniel again.

"Sure, Garrett," Daniel said. "I've heard of fun. I've heard of self-pity, too. And it seems to me you wallow in it like a pig in muck. Grow up, Noah. Your life isn't that bad."

"Oh, how would you know?" Noah spat out, the anger and embarrassment he felt building like a fire in dry leaves.

Suddenly, Noah was pinned up against the wall of the mess hall, and Daniel Stultz was in his face, right up against him, his elbow pushing hard into Noah's chest. His eyes were large and dark. "You want to know about fun, Garrett? I'll tell you about fun."

Boys came out of the other buildings, drawn by the sound of angry voices. They stood in the snow, watching.

"Fun," Daniel hissed, "is having cousins and an aunt and uncle you love dearly living in Poland when the Germans invade. Letters from them suddenly stop coming, and your letters to them are returned covered with useless foreign stamps that tell you nothing.

"Fun is when you finally find out from a family friend who managed to escape that they are living in a ghetto with barbed wire all around, just because they are Jewish.

"Fun is when that same friend, who ran for his life, informs you that your uncle was beaten to death for trying to steal food for his family.

"Fun is when you're told that just before this friend got out, your aunt was sick and would probably die since they were being denied medication along with food. Fun is realizing that now your little cousins may be alone and on their own.

"And here's a little more *fun* for you! Fun is knowing that they no longer even have the comfort of the ghetto but are in one of these camps!" Letting go of Noah, Daniel Stultz handed him a creased newspaper article from his pocket. Noah stared down at the headline, JEWS BEING ROUNDED UP AND EXTERMINATED IN CONCENTRATION CAMPS, under which was a picture of thousands of shoes, lying in a jumble. His stomach began to churn as he read about the mass killing of the owners of those shoes. Could this really be possible?

"Is *that* fun, Noah? How's that for *fun*?" Daniel Stultz shouted.

"I had no idea," Noah whispered. He looked over at the others, Wiley and Bill and Cam and Roger. They wouldn't meet his eyes, and he knew in that moment that they had known about these horrors.

"Yeah," Daniel said, "it's real fun trying to get you *idiots* to think of something besides yourselves.

"It's real *fun* hoping beyond hope that someone like you, Noah Garrett, can help me get back there and get my family out before they die like that" — he pointed to the article — "poisoned to death. So, yeah," Daniel finished, "I've heard of fun. But right now, fun is something I can't even *think* about until this war is over."

Then Daniel Stultz turned and walked away.

No one said a word. One by one, the boys began to drift back to their barracks as snow began to fall. For a long, long time, Noah stared down at the gruesome newspaper picture in his hands.

CHAPTER TWENTY

Noah could not concentrate at all the next day. He went through the motions, but his mind kept returning to that picture and the article. He didn't know how to reconcile being a pacifist with the horrors of what was being done to others in Europe.

Several times, he didn't place his piton the way Olaf had showed him, and he slid down the mountainside, scrambling wildly for a handhold.

"You are not using your head, Noah," Olaf reprimanded him.

Noah nodded and pushed the thoughts of his argument with Daniel to the back of his mind. But the thoughts wouldn't leave. Over and over, he kept hearing his parents saying, "Walk away, Noah," or "Turn the other cheek, Noah." And yet, there was that newspaper, and its horrible story and horrid picture. How could he not have known this was happening? And now what was he supposed to do about it?

"Concentrate. Concentrate," Olaf yelled, staring up at him from the foot of the mountain. "You must be able to do this vhen the time comes!"

Would the time come? Noah wondered. Would he go to war? Shouldn't *someone* be doing something to help those people? Shouldn't he? And yet the very idea of killing others, no matter the cause, sickened him and made him miss yet another step.

That night, he took his tray of food to a table away from Wiley and the others so he could be alone, but his uncle slid in next to him.

"I've had some time to think today, boy, after all that was said last night," his uncle said. "I can end this now, if you want. I'll go fess up to the general about your age. The truth will get you out of here and quick. It's up to you."

Noah looked at his uncle in surprise. He knew that if his uncle told the general the truth, James Shelley might be in trouble. Noah appreciated that his uncle was willing to risk that for him.

"I can promise you this, though," his uncle continued. "If you stay, I won't send you to war if you don't want. I'll make sure that doesn't happen. And if you should change your mind about fighting . . ." His uncle shrugged. "You'll have the training."

"If I left, where would I go?" Noah asked.

"You'd be a ward of the state, Noah," James Shelley answered, "at least until you're of legal age. I ain't got many friends outside of these guys here. And none of them would be willing to take on another mouth to feed."

Noah stared down at his plate. He still didn't know what the right thing to do was. But his uncle had promised not to send him to war if he didn't want to go. That, at least, had bought him some time to sort through these conflicting feelings he was having.

"I'll stay," Noah said.

His uncle let out his breath. "I'm glad."

Then he stood. The military man in him was back. "Get some sleep tonight. Starting tomorrow, you'll be joining the other boys for training. And we just got orders to head out at dawn for a three-week drill on Ptarmigan Peak. You'd best know, boy, this drill ain't going to be easy."

"I'll be ready," Noah told him, though his stomach suddenly felt queasy. Noah had seen Ptarmigan from the camp. He'd never been to the peak. The mountain wasn't steep, but it was high. The climb would be long, and the air would be thin. The only good thing about this three-week test was that it would get them all out of latrine duty.

"I know you won't let me down," his uncle added before he turned and walked away.

Knowing what was to come, Noah forced himself to finish his meal, in spite of his sick stomach. He had learned in the last eight weeks of training how important food and sleep were. You took them when you had the chance. You made the most of them.

When he was finished eating, he went outside, ready to head back to the barracks to try and get a decent night's sleep. But when he stepped outside the mess hall, he stopped.

The moon was rising, a full moon that lit up the mountains and made the night seem as clear and bright as day. The light twinkled off the snow, tumbling down the steep slope. It made a sparkling path right to the snow at Noah's feet.

Noah felt his heart lift at the sight. He was worried about tomorrow. He was unsure about *how* he would do. He was worried about the weeks to come. He was unsure about *what* he would do. But tonight, he could only see the beauty in front of him. He took a deep breath of the cold night air.

"You'll never be able to leave them again."

Noah turned to find Skeeter behind him. Skeeter grinned. "You're catching the bug, son. Once those mountains are in your heart, they're like a good woman — they'll stay there forever."

Noah looked back up at the mountains. He realized Skeeter was right. He was starting to love these mountains, in spite of the fact that he sometimes still longed for home and the heat and the tall grasses.

Skeeter pulled out a candy bar and ripped it open. He took a bite. "Shelley says you're going on the drill tomorrow."

Noah nodded.

"You nervous?" Skeeter asked.

"Yeah," Noah admitted.

Skeeter nodded. "I was, too, my first time. I thought I was the only one who was scared, but the funny thing was, I wasn't. Later, I found out that all the other recruits were just as nervous and scared as I was."

Noah laughed a little.

Skeeter took another bite out of his candy bar, then wrapped up the paper and shoved it into his shirt pocket. "Yeah, war's kind of like that, too. Everyone talks big. Everyone wants to go over and whip those Germans and Japanese and set them straight. But down deep, they're all scared. They're scared of dying, and they're scared of making someone else die. Sometimes, everyone wonders if what they're doing is right."

"Then how do you ever know, Skeeter?" Noah asked. "How do you know what's right and wrong?"

Skeeter stamped his feet in the snow. "Well, for me, it's like this. I stand out here, and I see those mountains. And I realize that I'm free to do whatever I want, to live a life as I choose. And I know that I can't stand by and not let other people have that same freedom."

Skeeter turned to look at Noah. "But it scares me just like everyone else, Noah. Some nights, it really shakes me up."

He stretched and yawned. "Oh well, it's a big day tomorrow. I'd better get some sleep."

He patted Noah on the shoulder and turned to walk away.

Noah watched Skeeter, crunching along in the snow, his shoulders hunched against the cold. Then he turned back to the mountains and the moon. The bright light shook and shimmered as the wind sent the snow up in huge swirls of white. There was no other sound.

But for once, Noah didn't feel alone. The mountains closed around him like old friends, and he felt comforted knowing that Skeeter was scared, too.

CHAPTER TWENTY-ONE

In the dark of the predawn day, Noah picked up his sack filled with ammunition and supplies and hoisted it onto his back. He strapped on his skis and joined the others heading out toward Ptarmigan Peak. As he began to ski up and out of Camp Hale, the fluttering in his stomach settled. He was one of the boys now. He would either shine on this drill, or he would flop. With Wiley, Bill, Cam, and Roger there beside him, Noah prayed it would not be the latter.

They were one long line of men in white — white parkas, white boots, white skis. As they rose higher into the mountains and the snow, the boys in front of Noah seemed to disappear, they blended in so easily with their surroundings.

Their food came behind them on toboggans pulled by skiers, and behind the toboggans were the mules carrying extra food and their artillery. In the quiet of the early morning, Noah could hear the animals' soft braying behind him even as his skis sliced a soft swooshing sound through the snow. Other than those two sounds, little was heard. Their orders were to ski out in silence, as if they were on a real mission, chasing a real enemy. Signals to change direction, to have someone take over leading the way, were given by hand.

By mid-morning, the temperature began dropping. Bill showed Noah how to rub bacon grease on his hands to prevent them from freezing, but even the grease could not stop his hands from stinging with cold when his wool gloves grew wet. Noah's back ached from the climb, but so far, he had no problem keeping up with the others. He felt strong and fit and proud of the job he was doing.

They took turns up front, breaking a trail in the snow for those behind them. This task was extremely difficult as the snow was knee-deep at these higher elevations. When Noah had finished his turn leading, his legs were shaking with fatigue, and he gladly signaled Wiley to take over for him. Before he made his way toward the back of the line, he looked down the mountain. Coming up the side of the mountain, boys skied in a crisscross fashion, like a snake writhing and crawling from side to side. Behind them came weasels, machines that rode up the mountain carrying Noah's uncle, Skeeter, Olaf, and Daniel, along with others who would serve as referees when the war games began. Noah envied his uncle the warmth of that vehicle.

When they reached the summit, they divided the entire outfit into two groups, separating them for the rest of the drill. Now there were enemies in the mountains, boys from the 85th and 87th, whom Noah would have to fight against as they trained.

Noah's group made camp that night in the snow. Fires weren't permitted, as they were training for warfare, and in enemy territory, fires could easily be spotted.

"Where are we supposed to go the bathroom?" Noah asked Wiley.

Wiley motioned Noah to follow him. A few hundred yards from where they had made camp, someone had dug a small trench in the snow and put a sign up that read LATRINE, 1944. Noah laughed out loud, glad that digging the trench wasn't going to be his punishment. Then he realized that he would have to strip off his pants and long underwear in order to use the improvised toilet. As he struggled with his clothes, Wiley, Bill, Roger, and Cam came to watch, laughing so hard at his efforts that tears came down the sides of their faces. When he had finished, Noah pulled his clothes back on and, with as much dignity as he could muster, strode past the boys.

They ate quickly and went to turn in for the night. Noah noticed that the others had taken pine boughs and laid them on their skis as a bed.

"What are you doing?" Noah asked. "Don't you want to use your tent?"

"We've bet each other we can spend the whole night outside," Wiley said, grinning. "You want to join in the challenge?"

Noah shook his head, wondering why in the world they would want to try something so crazy. After hours in the cold, who would choose to sleep outside when the warmth of a good tent was there for the taking? Noah set up his tent and laid out his sleeping bag, taking a little brush from his pack and sweeping the snow off him before crawling inside and going to sleep, pleased with his progress of that day.

In the morning, Noah sat up, relaxed and warm from a long dreamless sleep. He stretched his arms up overhead, yawning. His arm brushed the side of the tent.

"Holy —!" he yelled as a layer of snow and ice rained down upon him. He scrambled from the tent to find the guys waiting outside, laughing and slapping their thighs.

"Whoo ha!" Wiley laughed. "Problems there, Garrett?"

"Where did all that snow come from?" Noah shouted, brushing at his ice-encrusted hair and clothes.

"Your breath freezes to the wall of those tents. None of us use them now that we know about it. You're just lucky you didn't get showered in the middle of the night!" Bill sputtered as he struggled to talk between laughs.

"Yeah," Roger said, "we kept waiting to hear you scream. I was anticipating it so much, I hardly slept last night!"

"You could have warned me," Noah grumbled, shivering.

"Now, where's the fun in that?" Wiley said, grinning at him.

They all laughed again, and finally Noah joined in.

For the next week, they fought the other half of the boys of Camp Hale. Sometimes Noah's side won. Sometimes the others were victorious. Several times, Noah's heart nearly stopped as live ammunition whizzed past his head.

Boys who were captured by the other side came back and told stories of how real it had seemed, how they had been made to go without sleep for hours on end, until they were disoriented and shaky with fatigue.

There were no showers, and Noah's hair began to hang in greasy strands by his face. One week into maneuvers, Cam began to cough and then drew a fever. By the third day of hacking, he was diagnosed with pneumonia and sent back to camp. Noah watched him being taken from the mountain and almost envied him. The glory of joining the others and the confidence he was gaining in his skills began to wane, and he longed for a hot meal and a warm bed.

Several times, they were actually marched right through camp before ascending again into the mountains to take up another attack. Each time, Noah, Bill, Roger, and Wiley groaned seeing their barracks and remembering the comfort they offered as they skied back out and up.

In the second week, Noah found his feet swollen, and soon skin was peeling off them in great chunks.

"What the heck?" he said, as he tried to get the dead skin off and more kept forming.

"You've got trench foot," Bill said. "It's a fungus, and now you're stuck with it until maneuvers are over. You need to change your socks more often, Noah. Wet feet are what causes that."

Noah grimaced and tried not to think about it as he pulled on drier, warmer socks.

And yet, Noah could not say that he was unhappy. Sometimes, when the day was over, he would stand and watch the sunset, red rays shooting out from behind foamy clouds. In those moments, he would take a deep breath and see the beauty around him. He felt as if his parents were near, watching over him. And he thought again and again of the picture of those abandoned shoes and the stories of those destroyed lives in concentration camps. *They will never live to see this sight*, Noah thought. And he felt a sense of responsibility growing within him and was surprised by it.

On the day before Easter, as they once again approached the summit of Ptarmigan Peak for the end of their three-week drill, the temperature dropped precipitously. The next morning, a late spring blizzard hit. They could barely see in front of them.

Noah's rifle didn't work during maneuvers. It had frozen in the cold.

The snow came so fast and so deep that the mules were unable to get through. For the rest of the drill, they would have little food. Noah's stomach growled loudly in his ears as he skied onward. *Is this what war is like?* he wondered. *Or is it* worse?

Halfway through the day, the general halted their progress.

"We've got to wait for some stretchers," he said. "I got two men in there with frostbite and one burning with fever."

It was Noah's turn to lead the way when they started up again. He blazed a trail for his comrades in the deepening snow, throwing hand grenades at the slopes that were too dangerous to ski. The controlled explosions sent the snow tumbling down, making the slopes less steep and less likely to cause an avalanche. Slowly, he led the others toward the peak.

At one point, Noah's uncle pulled up beside him in his Weasel, its engine roaring loudly. "You all right?"

Noah simply nodded. He needed to save all his energy for the climb.

"You're doing a great job there, boy," his uncle added before driving off.

In the late afternoon, the light, dry snow that was falling became heavy and wet. It clung to Noah's uniform, soaking him completely. He shivered with the cold. When they stopped for the night, the general sent back more boys with frostbite and illness. He ordered everyone to take the newly fallen snow and build themselves an igloo. They would camp here if the blizzard was still raging tomorrow.

Noah was exhausted, but welcomed the warmth the igloo would provide and the hint of a few days' rest. He and Wiley packed the snow tightly, building block upon block until they had a snug shelter in which to hunker down for a few days. At one point, Roger threw a snowball at them, but Wiley and Noah were too tired to take up the challenge.

James Shelley came by at supper to check in on Noah and take a meal with him.

Just as they were all about to turn in, a report of a downed pilot in trouble near Ptarmigan Peak was heard over the radio.

"Can we get to him?" Noah asked.

Olaf shook his head. "No. There is nothing ve can do. The snows and drifts are too strong. Ve are used to this veather and these conditions. Pilots are not. The pilot von't make it, I'm afraid."

Noah felt sick, thinking about the pilot, possibly hurt, and unable to get help, slowly freezing to death up on the mountain.

Quietly, everyone turned in that night. There seemed little to say.

Noah woke the next morning to find his clothes frozen to him. Stiffly, he went outside to find a glorious day, the snow over and the sun shining brightly. For once, he wished for more snow, for he knew that now they would be off again. And sure enough, the order was given to break camp.

Noah strapped on his skis, picked up his pack, and set off with the others up the mountain.

But a short distance out, there was a sudden cry, and the troop was ordered to halt. The general came skiing up the slope, stopping every so often and asking questions. When he reached Noah, he pulled up beside him. Noah paused, his throat suddenly tight. Had the general found out about him?

"Where's your uncle?" the general asked.

"What?" Noah said, confused.

"Has anyone seen James Shelley?" the general called out.

Noah waited while the word was passed back among the ranks. He felt a sudden sense of foreboding.

James Shelley did not step forward. It seemed as if Noah's uncle had simply disappeared.

CHAPTER TWENTY-TWO

In the three days that followed, blizzard conditions set in again and did not let up. Noah continued to ski out each morning with the others and engage in war games, hoping his uncle would reappear at day's end. But there was no sign of James Shelley.

Finally, the maneuvers were over, and they were all ordered back to camp. The boys fell exhausted into their beds. Noah dozed occasionally and then fitfully.

No search party could be sent for James Shelley until the snow let up. Noah felt helpless and angry as he watched the bad weather continue. Skeeter forced him to eat, though the food was tasteless, and he only did it so that he wouldn't find himself too sleepy to stay awake.

The other boys crept around him. No one said anything, but there was a general sense of doom in the air.

On the second night after their return, Noah paced the

barracks, back and forth, back and forth, hoping for daylight and the end of the storm.

"Noah?" Wiley's voice was soft and low. "You need to give it a break, buddy. You need to get some sleep."

"Why?" Noah snapped. "Is it just that I'm keeping *you* awake?"

There was an embarrassed silence.

"Actually," Bill said into the darkness, "yes."

"But it's all right, Noah," Cam put in quickly. "We understand."

Noah didn't wait to hear any more. He left the warmth of the barracks, slamming the door behind him and making his way through the swirling, heavy snow, cursing it as he stomped through the camp. He knew the boys were right. His walking back and forth across the squeaky wooden floors of the barracks all night long would irritate him, too, if the roles were reversed. But the fact that they mentioned *wanting* to sleep just reminded Noah that he would be the one most affected if James Shelley didn't return. And as more time passed, Noah was aware that this was a good possibility. He knew he should be worried about what would happen to him but, strangely, all he could think of was his uncle. He was worried about him. His uncle was irritating and completely the opposite of Noah's parents, yet Noah began to realize that if Shelley didn't ever come back, he would actually miss the gruff, cantankerous man.

When he reached the barn, he went inside, letting the heat of the animals and the smell of fresh hay calm him a bit. In the dark, he made his way to the first stall, crooning softly. "Hey, boy. Hey, boy."

He could hear several of the mules shuffle in their stalls. The animal nearest him came forward and put his head over the half door. Noah rubbed his hand along the mule's soft nose and scratched the animal behind his ears, hoping for some sense of peace to ease the constant tension he'd felt since Shelley's disappearance. "How are you there, boy?"

The door to the barn opened, and Noah turned to see Daniel silhouetted in the beam of a flashlight, snow coming down behind him. Noah's heart thumped deep in his chest. It was bad enough to have been caught talking to mules, but now, here was Daniel Stultz discovering it. How much worse could one day get?

Daniel came into the barn, shutting the door behind him. His flashlight bobbed dark shadows about as he walked over. "Wiley thought you might be mad at him and the boys. He was afraid you might be tempted to do something foolish."

"So he sent you?" Noah asked. Wiley didn't even like Daniel Stultz, and he'd been there when Noah had had it out with Daniel three weeks ago!

Daniel shrugged. "Actually, he tried to find Skeeter first. I just happened along and offered to help. I thought you might be here."

Noah swallowed hard, thinking about their fight before the maneuvers and some of the things Noah had unwittingly said.

"Don't know why you'd bother about me," Noah muttered, "not after the way I went after you the other day."

Daniel raised an eyebrow. "Are you apologizing, Garrett?"

Noah hesitated. "Yes. Although it's not a particularly good apology, I guess."

Daniel snorted.

Noah took a deep breath, all the embarrassment and confusion he'd felt over their confrontation choking him. He knew he had to make things right with Daniel. "I'm sorry. I really am. I feel stupid. I didn't know what the Nazis were doing to Jews over there. And now, to know that your family is stuck in those camps" — Noah met Daniel's stare — "that must be really hard."

"Don't sweat it, Garrett," Daniel said.

"But . . . ," Noah began uncertainly.

"Look," Daniel interrupted, "nobody in this country knew what was happening over there because the *press* didn't feel like letting them know. The story was too . . ." He paused. "Ugly," he finally spat out.

Noah didn't know what to say.

"That picture I showed you?" Daniel asked.

Noah nodded.

"It just came out! For months, the press has been burying the story *deep* in the pages of our illustrious papers!" Daniel said.

"I'm sorry," Noah whispered.

Daniel gave a harsh laugh. "I didn't realize it was *your* fault, Garrett. Are you a secret Nazi or something?"

Noah looked at him. "Still, to think about your family, trapped . . . I can't imagine facing every day knowing that."

Daniel didn't respond, and Noah wondered if he'd said too much.

"The waiting must be the worst," Noah ventured again.

Daniel gave another snort of laughter. "Kind of funny, isn't it, Garrett? I'm probably the only one here who knows how you're feeling right about now."

Noah blinked with surprise at the truth of Daniel's observation.

Daniel cleared his throat. "Your uncle is a fine soldier, Garrett. If anyone can survive those mountains and this storm, it's Shelley."

"And if he doesn't make it?" Noah asked, his voice shaking.

Daniel's eyes flashed. "Are you going to go soft on him now, Garrett?"

Noah shuffled his feet uncomfortably. Daniel was right. He was acting like a baby. His uncle would have hated that.

Daniel reached in his pocket and withdrew a carrot. He held it out to the mule, and the animal quickly snatched it away. Daniel rubbed the animal's nose for a minute.

"Shelley said you were from the Bronx," Noah said. "So what is with you and the carrots?"

Daniel didn't say anything.

"They got lots of mules in the city now?" Noah joked.

"My family . . . ," Daniel said abruptly. He stopped, pursed his lips. "My family lives in the Bronx, but I went to school at Dartmouth." He smiled ruefully. "Or at least I used to."

Noah let out a low whistle. "Dartmouth? Gee, you must be smart."

"What made you think I wasn't smart?" Daniel asked.

Noah felt himself redden.

Daniel sighed. "I miss school, especially the classes. I had hoped to teach classical studies some day."

"You probably still can," Noah said. "It's not like you can't go back later."

Daniel laughed. "If there is a later. If I'm not dead at the end of this war."

Noah didn't know how to respond to Daniel's statement. What he said was true. "Did you learn how to deal with animals at school? Dartmouth's in the country, isn't it?"

Daniel watched the mule chewing for a moment. "A little. But mostly, I learned about it at my uncle's farm in Poland when I was little and we went to visit — long before the invasion."

Noah thought about how awful it must be for Daniel to envision his aunt suffering and dying, his uncle being beaten by soldiers, and his little cousins being shipped off to a concentration camp with barbed wire and guns.

"Coming here," Daniel continued, "helps me remember them. It helps me remember what I'm doing here."

Quiet settled over the barn.

"It helps me remember, too," Noah agreed.

Daniel looked at the floor of the barn.

"It sure is tough, though," Noah said, his voice gruff with the emotion he was trying to hold back, "this waiting, this hoping. Since my parents died, I have a hard time believing anything will be right again."

"But," Daniel said, his voice cracking, too, "holding on to hope is the only thing that's left."

Noah glanced over and saw that Daniel's eyes were wet. He

looked quickly away. He would not let Daniel Stultz know that he had seen his tears.

"So now, Garrett," Daniel said, as he stood up straight and wiped his hands on his pants, "as your commanding officer, I order you to go and get some sleep. Is that understood?"

Noah nodded. "Yes, sir!"

Daniel turned to leave. "And, Garrett," he added in a soft voice over his shoulder, "no matter what, continue to hold on to that hope. 'Cause there's nothing either of us can do right now, anyway, but that."

Noah woke to shouting in the camp. "Someone's coming. Someone's coming down off the mountain."

Noah was up and off like a shot. Boys were gathered at the far end of the camp, peering into the swirling snow.

Noah stared hard into the blanket of white. But he couldn't tell if the man coming slowly down the mountainside was his uncle or not.

Skeeter came and stood by him. "Somebody go get me a pair of binoculars!"

Noah couldn't just stand there and wait to see who the person coming down out of the mountains was. He ran to the barracks and got his skis. He strapped them on, and ignoring Skeeter, who yelled at him to stop, headed off toward the slope, skiing out hard and fast. Higher and higher he rose, keeping his eyes on the figure coming down. Snow pelted him. The wind blew him from side to side.

But at last, he could see. It was his uncle!

Noah skied up to him, stopping just short of James Shelley. He could feel tears streaming down his face, freezing on his cheeks. He stopped himself short of trying to embrace his uncle.

"Jesus," Shelley mumbled, his words sounding like the words of a drunken man, "stop that confounded crying, Noah Garrett, and get this monkey off my back, will you?"

Noah looked more closely, and then he saw. Slung on his uncle's shoulder was a man. Stiffly, James Shelley pulled the man around and handed to Noah the pilot who'd been left for dead.

CHAPTER TWENTY-THREE

When they arrived back at camp, Noah's uncle collapsed. Both he and the pilot were taken to the hospital barracks to be treated. Noah trotted along behind them, determined not to leave his uncle's side.

"He has pneumonia," the doctor pronounced after examining James Shelley.

Noah's uncle tossed and turned, moaning loudly.

"His fever's very high," the doctor added, shaking his head.

Noah sat by his uncle's bed, washing away the beads of sweat that were on his forehead. "He's not going to die, is he?"

"I don't know, son," the doctor replied. "It's a bad case, and your uncle is weak from his time on the mountain. They're sending us a new drug soon called penicillin that someone developed to deal with pneumonia. I'll give it to your uncle when it arrives and maybe it will help. But I've never used it before so I don't know how he'll respond."

Noah felt as if he couldn't breathe. He hadn't prayed since his parents died. Now he prayed again. He prayed long and hard.

It couldn't happen, he kept thinking. It just couldn't happen to him again.

The fever raged on for three weeks. James Shelley thrashed around, throwing his limbs wildly from side to side. He muttered in his sleep, and in his delirium spat out incoherent words and strange phrases. Noah tried not to notice when the doctor left each day after checking on him. He had given James Shelley the penicillin when it finally arrived, but still his eyebrows were knit with worry.

Wiley, Bill, Cam, and Roger came to see him. Cam brought cookies his mother had sent, and Wiley told funny stories about things he'd heard people had muttered when they were delirious with fever. The stories made the others laugh, and Noah tried to join in but just couldn't. They each offered to sit with Shelley while Noah got some sleep. Noah thanked them but did not take them up on their offer. He stayed right beside his uncle. If he was tired, he slept in the chair by the bed. Skeeter often slept in a chair beside him when his duties for the day were over.

Even Daniel came by, bringing hot food for Noah and sitting with him while he tried to eat. When Noah finished and Daniel stood to leave, he put his hand on Noah's shoulder. "I told you he would make it."

"But will he survive?" Noah asked in anguish as he looked at his uncle, so still and almost deathlike.

"Remember what I said in the barn, Noah," Daniel reminded him as he left.

Noah looked back at his uncle. The man drank excessively sometimes. He was wild and boorish and hung out with questionable folks. But Noah knew he still cared about him, in spite of all that. And so he would do as Daniel said. He'd hold on to that hope.

A week later, Noah roused suddenly, his head having fallen onto his chest as he slept. The bed in front of him was empty!

Noah jumped from the chair, his heart thumping wildly. He looked around. The sick ward was empty, too.

Had his uncle died in his sleep? Had they taken his dead uncle's body from the building without even waking Noah?

Then he heard the sound of a toilet flushing, and the door to the bathroom swung open. James Shelley stood unsteadily in the doorway, his face white and drawn.

"Did the pilot make it?" he demanded.

Noah almost choked with relief at seeing that his uncle's fever had broken. "Yes, sir."

A slight smile touched Shelley's lips, replaced by a frown just as quickly. "Why aren't you out training, boy? You go soft on me while I was recovering in here?"

Noah grinned. "My assigned duty is to watch over you."

"I don't need no darn babysitter," James Shelley argued, but his voice was weak.

"General's orders," Noah told him. "You're stuck with me."

"Then what are you standing there for?" his uncle demanded. "Help me to the darn bed."

Noah blinked back tears of gratitude, and silently prayed his thanks at the return of the surly man he had come to know and like.

Each day, James Shelley got better. Each day, he got grouchier. By the end of two weeks, he was back to his old self.

"I want a drink!" he roared at the doctor. "I just came down from the most horrendous ski of my life, and I need something to calm my nerves."

"I'm going to tell you the same thing I've told you every day this week, James Shelley," the doctor said, unperturbed. "You've just pulled through pneumonia. You're on medication, medication that doesn't mix with alcohol. Now, unless you're really determined to do yourself in, you're just going to have to wait a week or two to have that drink."

"A week?" James Shelley roared. "I have to wait a week or two?"

Later they set a tray of food down in front of him. He peered at it.

"What is this crap?" he asked. "Baby food again? I keep telling them I want a real meal, not this wimpy toast and tea. I want steak and eggs."

Noah stifled a laugh.

"Come here, boy," James Shelley called. "Run over to the mess hall. Get them to rustle me up some real grub. I can't eat this. I need more than toast and jam to keep this big body going."

Noah nodded and left the hospital. Outside, the camp was foot-deep in mud. The snow was melting. Spring had fully arrived while Noah sat pent up with his sick uncle.

Skeeter came up beside Noah. "He can be a real pain when he's confined, can't he?"

Noah smiled. "Yeah, he's been running me all around since he started feeling better."

Skeeter laughed. "Don't worry. I heard the doctor say another two days or so and he'll be back training again. He'll just have to stay on the medication for a bit longer." Skeeter motioned with his head. "Why don't you take a few hours off? I'll go sit with him awhile."

"Thanks. Do you mind getting him some food first, though?"

Skeeter laughed. "Sure thing." He began to head toward the mess hall.

"Hey, Skeeter?"

Skeeter turned.

"Do you ever get confused between what a person says and how they act?" Noah asked.

"You mean your uncle?"

Noah nodded.

"There's never only one side to anyone, Noah," Skeeter said. "There's a good side and a dark side in all of us. I suppose with your uncle it's just easier to see both sides. Most people hide one side or the other."

Skeeter sighed. "Nah, nothing in this world's ever black and white. But, Lord, wouldn't it be nice if it was?"

"Yeah," Noah said. "Maybe then I'd understand how my uncle can be so tough on me sometimes and so nice to me at others."

Skeeter smiled. "He's a good man, Noah. And maybe that's all you need to understand."

A week later, Noah was back training with the boys. After a day of rock training, balancing his way across wet logs and huge boulders, Noah went to look for Shelley. He was hungry and excited to tell his uncle about the day. He'd beat everyone across and hadn't fallen once, though Wiley had, more times than Noah could count.

"Have you seen Shelley?" he asked one of the boys passing him.

"Yeah. He was headed toward the general's office."

Noah took off in that direction. As he neared the general's office, he heard raised voices.

"I can't do it!" the general was yelling. "I really can't."

"You've got to!" James Shelley insisted. "We've got to find a way!"

Noah peered curiously into the general's office. His uncle was sitting in a chair with his back to the door. The general was pacing back and forth.

"You shouldn't have lied to me, Shelley," the general said. "You just shouldn't have."

Noah's uncle shrugged. "Okay, okay. I'm sorry. I know I never should have had Dana get me a fake birth certificate for the kid, but what else did you expect me to do with him? Send him to an orphanage?"

"He could have been killed out there on maneuvers," the general snapped. "That's no place for a fifteen-year-old."

"He'll be sixteen in two months. Besides, he ain't bad, is he?" James Shelley said, grinning.

The general sighed. "Yeah, he's pretty good. Actually, he's really good on the ropes, and his skiing is improving, too."

Then the general started pacing again. "But that's beside the point. We're moving to Texas now. Our time may be coming, Shelley. The Germans have finally been pushed back into Europe, and the military wants us trained in the maneuvers every army unit gets, so they're sending us to Camp Swift. Things will be different there, more serious, more rules and regulations. I can't have a kid with us, not until he's sixteen. He just can't go. I can't do it."

Noah suddenly felt a lump in his throat. His head pounded.

Noah's uncle was silent a moment. "You've got to find a way, General. I want that kid with me."

"And if we go overseas?" the general asked. "What then?"

"I'll go back to his hometown while we're in Texas, or I'll talk to one of the military wives," his uncle replied. "I'll find someone to watch him while I'm there. He just won't be in any orphanage, see, 'cause it won't be permanent or anything."

The general shook his head. "I'm sorry, Shelley, but you can't. He can't live in the barracks down there."

"Then get me into married housing," his uncle said. "They got kids there, don't they?"

"Married housing?" the general hooted. "How do you expect to survive that, Shelley? You'll hate it."

"Just do it," Noah's uncle said, standing. "He's the only family I got left, General, and maybe in the past that didn't mean much to me. But I'm getting older, and it seems it does now. So, you gotta do it for me."

The general stopped pacing and looked at Noah's uncle. "You've really gone soft for the kid, Shelley."

"I have not," Noah's uncle insisted. "He's just family, like I said, that's all."

The general grinned. Then he waved a hand. "Okay, okay. All this incredible sentimentality from you makes me feel like throwing up. I'll get you into married housing. I just hope that kid appreciates what you're doing for him."

Noah scrambled away from the door and around to the back of the barracks. He didn't want his uncle to know he'd been spying on him.

He leaned against the side of the building, feeling the warmth of the wood, and thought about what he'd heard. His uncle had said Noah mattered. He was willing to give up his way of life for him. And that woman, Dana — if it wasn't for her, Noah would have been sent to an orphanage long ago. All these thoughts crowded his mind.

He waited a minute or two and then came back around the side of the barracks. He was going to find his uncle. He'd tell him the truth. He'd tell him that he'd heard everything, and he'd thank him. His uncle deserved that. It was time he saw that Noah was truly grateful for what he'd done.

He could see James Shelley already ahead of him, striding down the road of the camp. Noah ran to catch up. But just as he reached him, a man on crutches stepped out from the door of the hospital. It was the pilot. Noah stopped in his tracks.

The pilot hobbled slowly up to James Shelley.

"Well," Noah's uncle said, "looks like you're doing okay and ready for action."

The pilot grinned and nodded. "Yeah. Thanks to you all I lost was a few toes and not my life."

The pilot ran a hand through his hair. "Look. I want to thank you —"

James Shelley interrupted. "Stop, stop, stop. None of that now. I just did what I've been trained to do, that's all. Go back to bed, soldier. You're looking a little wobbly still."

The pilot hesitated and then nodded. He stood straight and smartly saluted James Shelley. Then he turned and went back inside the hospital, closing the door behind him.

Noah stood and watched his uncle move away, farther down the road of the camp. Noah didn't go after him. He didn't know how to express to his uncle what he felt for him in a way his uncle would accept. How did he tell this reticent man that he had come to respect him and, in a strange way, care about him?

CHAPTER TWENTY-FOUR

Camp Swift was forty miles from Austin, Texas. And, Noah soon discovered, a million miles from Camp Hale. While their lives at Camp Hale had been hard from a training standpoint, the rules had been lax. But at Camp Swift, law and order were strictly maintained.

They were truly preparing for war now. On June 6, the Allies had hit the beaches in Normandy, driving the Germans deep into France. The tension and excitement over that victory were apparent everywhere at Camp Swift.

Noah and his uncle were housed with the married officers, and Noah was banned from training. Noah's uncle grumbled every day. "Doggone, stupid idiots. It's one hundred and two in the shade, and they got me in ties and shoes that have to be shined."

Then he'd turn on Noah. "You know how lucky you are, boy? We gotta stand all day long in the heat. We gotta march up and down and down and up. We gotta shoot rifles and dig foxholes in this confounded weather."

Noah smiled. He remembered his first attempt at foxhole digging.

His uncle leaned down off the bed and grabbed something running across the floor. "And they got these lizards here. And snakes, too. And Skeeter has poison oak so bad, he can't open his left eye. How'd you ever stand it in a place like this?"

"I don't know, Uncle Shelley," Noah said. "This wasn't exactly what I remembered."

"So, your memory's faulty, eh?" his uncle said, stamping toward the door. "Well, see you tonight." He threw the door open. "If I survive the heat, that is."

And he was gone.

His uncle was right. Texas wasn't at all what Noah remembered. He had finally gotten what he'd wanted. He'd come home. He was only twenty miles from where he had been born and raised, but it could have been the other side of the world. Noah didn't feel right at all.

He moved idly around the house. Two weeks ago, Noah's birthday had come and gone. With sugar in short supply, there had been no cake. And with everyone training so hard, there had been no party. He had turned sixteen.

Still, he had not officially signed up of his own accord. So Noah spent his days alone, feeling at loose ends. They had a little house, one among thousands of rows of married housing. All the houses looked the same and were painted the same color, a light pink. Oftentimes, Noah got confused and went into some-one else's house. He hated how everything looked the same.

There was a pool and a theater nearby and other kids, too, children of the enlisted married men. But he couldn't bring himself to make friends with them.

Noah had changed. His mind was still in the mountains. At night, he dreamed of skiing, of rock climbing, of scaling a granite wall. And during the day, he just kept thinking of how hot it was. On the walls of his room, Noah kept pinups of mountains from the camp newspaper, the *Blizzard*. The paper was the joke of the army. While other military papers had a pinup girl in each issue, the *Blizzard* had a pinup mountain. Noah waited each week to see which mountain would be featured and was always elated when it was one of the mountains he had scaled or skied.

He ran. He ran ten to twelve miles in the hot summer heat. He ran up into the hills near the camp, and among the brush weed that surrounded married housing. When he came back from running, he swam two miles in the pool, while other boys near his age splashed and played beside him and ogled the officers' daughters. He couldn't seem to join in.

At night, his uncle would come and get him and take him back to join the others in the single men's barracks. Noah had become a celebrity. Everyone was proud of what he had accomplished back at Camp Hale, now knowing that he had only been fifteen. Wiley, Cam, Roger, and Bill cheered each time he entered the mess hall. Even Daniel offered him a smile. It wasn't enough. He missed being with them. He missed the unit. He missed the mountains. At night, he would sit with the rest of the 85th, 86th, and 87th, watch color slides of alpine scenes, and wish himself back there.

Noah knew he wasn't the only one suffering. They all were. But it was different for him. He was home now. It shouldn't have felt so strange.

When he ran and swam, he thought. And his thoughts just confused him more. Who was he? The Texas farm boy who'd left Austin after his parents' death? Or the mountain boy who'd found a passion he'd never thought he had?

Noah thought about what his uncle had said. How *had* he ever lived or felt comfortable here?

Then an idea came to him, a crazy idea, but one that might settle some questions for him.

It would be a long run, but he could hike part of the way. He figured it would take him all day, maybe even into the night. But Noah didn't care. Just the possibility that he could find some answers filled him with hope and determination.

So one dry, hot morning, Noah picked up a few canteens and filled them with water. He packed a knapsack with food. He wrote his uncle a note, telling him where he'd gone and that he'd be back in a day or two.

Then Noah strapped on the rucksack and headed out of the house. He closed the door behind him. He was headed for home.

Noah could see the house from a distance, rising out of the tall grasses, the flattened fields. He was tired. It had taken him longer than he had expected. He had spent the night on the ground.

As he neared the white farmhouse, he slowed. He could feel his heart pounding. At the bottom of the steps to the front porch, he stopped, hesitant to go farther. But the house was empty, the FOR SALE sign fallen to the ground.

Noah went up onto the front porch, pushed open the door, and walked in. His footsteps echoed through the halls and rooms. Immediately, memories came flooding back.

He remembered dinners together, he and his mother and father always sitting in the exact same chairs every night. He remembered Saturday night checkers games with his father and summer afternoons drinking lemonade in front of the fan with his mother. He remembered waking to the sound of his father's tractor.

And he began to feel good again, safe and warm. He remembered what it was like to have a home. And in the stillness, he could hear his voice and his mother's and father's, all laughing together. It seemed wrong that the place was so abandoned.

Noah walked around the house and then stepped out back. The sun blinded him for a minute, and then he saw his parents' gravestones, standing just as he remembered.

Noah picked some wildflowers and laid them at the base of the stones.

"Hi, Ma," he whispered. "Hi, Pa."

The wind whistled through the grasses. Noah felt his parents there, with him now. He sensed they were close. He felt sure in that moment that they could hear him, and that they wanted him to speak.

"I'm okay," he said aloud, feeling a bit silly. "Uncle Shelley's been taking real good care of me."

Noah sat down. He reached out and let his fingers brush his mother's name, carved in stone.

"Ma?" he whispered. "I'm real confused, about this war, about fighting. And about how someone like Uncle Shelley, who's so different from what you taught me to be, can be such a good man. Because he is, Mama. He really is. He's a good man.

"And Pa," Noah continued, turning to his father's stone, "I wish you could help me with what kind of man I should be, because I just don't know. I just don't know who I am or where I belong in all this.

"I just wish you hadn't gone. I wish I knew why it had to be time for you both to go," Noah finished.

Noah felt something heavy on his shoulder and turned to find his uncle standing behind him. In the driveway, Noah could see a jeep. He hadn't even heard the vehicle pull in.

"Jeesh, boy," his uncle said, "you scared the living daylights out of me, leaving that way."

"I had to come home," Noah said.

"Yeah," his uncle replied. "I can see that."

Noah looked up at his uncle. "Uncle Shelley, I'm real confused."

His uncle nodded. "I know, Noah boy. I heard you. You don't know where you belong now, and I know that feeling 'cause I've been there. It wasn't easy when I left home. I wasn't sure I'd done the right thing. Even now, I'm not sure if I did what was best. But I've learned something from you, Noah."

Noah looked at his uncle questioningly.

"Look around," James Shelley commanded.

Noah did. He saw the grasses and the flatness and the sameness of it all.

"This here," his uncle said, "this is your childhood, safe, secure, predictable.

"And the mountains," he continued, "they're your future. 'Cause you know, boy, life ain't flat and plain. It's convoluted, with twists and turns and dangers that no one can know. But at the same time, it can take your breath away, it's so darn beautiful."

"But how come I feel funny here now?" Noah asked.

Noah's uncle sighed. "Because it's behind you, Noah. Just like my past is behind me now, whether it was right to leave or not. But don't worry. It's still a part of both of us. And it always will be. It's what gives us the strength to face the mountains, Noah. It's what will give you the foundation to face life."

Noah turned and looked out over the fields. A hawk rose high in the air, turning and spiraling.

Noah turned back to his uncle. Skeeter was right. "Uncle Shelley," he began.

His uncle held up his hand. "Aw, come on. Please don't say it. I'm not an idiot. You're my biggest fan now. I get it. Let's leave it at that, okay?" He began walking back toward the jeep. "Come on. I've got to get back."

Noah sighed. He would never be able to tell James Shelley he cared about him. But Shelley knew, and maybe that was good enough. Noah looked one more time at his parents' gravestones. He guessed he had his parents' answer. They had sent his uncle to him yet again. And Shelley was right. Wherever he went, his life in Texas would be a part of him. But it could no longer be all of him. It was time to move on.

Noah stood up and headed toward his uncle and the jeep, knowing that in taking those last steps away from here, he was finally letting the past go.

CHAPTER TWENTY-FIVE

Skeeter was waiting for them when they returned. "We're leaving, Shelley. Orders are to move to Virginia beginning of November."

"Virginia?" James Shelley said.

Skeeter nodded. "I've heard we won't be there long before we'll be shipping out. Now that the Allies are in France and the Germans are fighting hard in Italy and Germany itself, they need every last man here to finally end this thing."

Noah's uncle turned to look at Noah. "Guess I knew this moment would come sometime, boy. Looks like we'll be parting ways soon."

Noah's heart sank.

"When we first got here, I arranged for you to stay with one of these military families on base," his uncle continued. "Guess we'd best be about introducing you to them tomorrow."

"But where are you being sent?" Noah said. "Won't they tell you?"

Skeeter shook his head. "We won't know until we're on board ship. They want to maintain secrecy as long as possible."

"But what if they send you to Germany?" Noah asked, trying to keep the panic from his voice.

"Then we go to Germany, boy," Noah's uncle said. "We do as we're ordered. You know that."

Skeeter laughed. "Don't worry about your uncle. His hide's too tough to shoot through. And the Germans will give him back if they ever get him. They wouldn't want him."

Noah's uncle guffawed. "See, Noah boy, nothing to worry about."

Noah just nodded, but in that moment, he thought back to what his uncle had said to him just a few hours ago. His past was behind him, but the future of his uncle and others like him was now in the balance. Noah could no longer hide. He may not believe in fighting, but he did believe in family. It was time to face the mountain.

Noah walked in late the next morning to find his uncle and Skeeter waiting for him.

"Where have you been?" his uncle roared. "I thought I told you we had to go this morning to see those folks who agreed to take you. I got to get you settled before I ship outta here. I don't need to be worrying about you right now."

"Calm down, Shelley," Noah said quietly.

"Calm down?" James Shelley roared. "Calm down? Who are you to tell me to calm down?"

"One of your boys," Noah said. "I'm one of the boys who will be sailing with you to wherever."

"What in Sam Hill are you talking about, Noah?" his uncle said, his eyes suddenly narrowing.

"I guess you forgot I'm sixteen, old enough to sign up," Noah said. "I'm going with you, Shelley. I enlisted with the Phantoms."

After the initial shock wore off, Noah's uncle went crazy. "You need permission to sign up when you're only sixteen! You haven't got permission."

Noah laughed. "Yes, I do. You already signed permission when we were at Camp Hale."

"But I was lying," his uncle fumed.

"But only the general and the boys in the division know that. Want me to tell the authorities *here*?" Noah asked. "Then maybe you'd be court-martialed and unable to go. We could both stay home."

Noah's uncle's eyes bulged with anger.

Skeeter yanked Noah outside before his uncle really started shouting.

"I don't see what he's so worked up about," Noah muttered, as Skeeter hurried him out of sight. "He did some crazy things when he was my age."

Skeeter sighed. "He's just scared, Noah. He doesn't want you near the fighting."

"I just want to be with him," Noah protested.

"I know that's what you want, Noah," Skeeter said. "But your uncle loves you. He doesn't want you hurt. He *knows* you only signed up to be with him. And the bottom line is this: You've only just turned sixteen, and you've been raised a pacifist. And while I'll be the first to admit that you could hold your own with the best of us, you're still a kid, a kid who doesn't really understand the world yet and who doesn't believe in war. You deserve to grow up a little more before you do something like this."

"But I *am* grown up, Skeeter," Noah argued. "I feel funny with the officers' kids here. I belong with you guys and with my uncle."

Skeeter smiled slightly. "Yeah, I bet you feel funny, Noah. You've grown up fast. But in a war, there's more growing up to do. And nobody wants you growing up that fast."

Noah didn't say anything, but for a moment, he felt a twinge of doubt. Had he made a mistake by signing up?

Twelve weeks later, Noah stood looking at the SS *Argentina* as it lay in the harbor the day they were to set sail from Virginia to join the war effort. A chilly December wind blew off the water. Enlisting had seemed like the absolute right thing to do that distant morning in Texas. But now that the time had come for them to actually head for combat, Noah's stomach felt odd and his mouth strangely dry.

The dress uniform he wore was scratchy and overstarched, and the patches they'd just received with a mountain and two crossed rifles too stiff. They were no longer the 85th, 86th, and 87th. They had a brand-new name to go with their deployment — the Tenth Mountain Division. Noah had stood for a long time in front of the mirror when he had first put the uniform on this morning. The boy who had stared back at him looked calm and ready, a true soldier. Noah wished he felt as confident as he looked.

He gazed out at the ocean, wondering what he would find over there, wondering where they were going, wondering if he would even be alive at the end of this war to return to Texas or the mountains or anywhere else in the United States.

Two sailors walked up the gangplank, laughing and carrying canvas bags slung over their shoulders.

"Yeah," one said, "we're taking a bunch of skiers on board. Imagine that!"

"Skiers?" the other asked. "What division are they with?"

The first one shrugged. "Some group named the Tenth Mountain Division. But I hear people call them the Phantoms."

"Phantom skiers, huh?" The other sailor laughed. .

"Yeah." The first sailor chuckled. "Sounds crazy to me, too, but I hear they've got some good poker players, so maybe the trip won't be a total bust."

The two sailors laughed again and headed onto the boat.

Noah watched them go, feeling even more uneasy. Not only was he sailing away toward war and battles, but he was sailing with a group of soldiers who were the laughingstock of the military. They were skiers. What *could* they do?

A hand landed on Noah's shoulder. His uncle stood beside him. He hadn't spoken much to Noah even after he calmed down about Noah's enlisting. The rest of the unit and Skeeter and the general were with him. They all stood looking at the SS *Argentina.*

"Well," James Shelley finally said, "let's load up and go to war."

The boat was cramped, and Wiley and Cam were seasick from the beginning. Everyone was jittery, talking too much or not talking at all. Everyone wanted to know where they were headed and what their mission would be, but secrecy was still being maintained.

Noah didn't say much, either. Although he felt fine, the closeness of the ship and the strangeness of actually leaving the United States for the first time in his life made the trip seem almost unreal to him. And while he liked watching the water crash into the boat as they made their way, he wished it were a pleasure voyage he was on and not one so fraught with danger.

After two days at sea, the intercom suddenly sprang to life, and the general's voice rang out loud and clear. "Well, boys, it's safe to tell you now. How many of you would like to know where this boat is headed?"

There was a sudden hush. Even Wiley and Cam sat up, color rushing to their white faces.

"Italy," the general called out. "We're going to Italy, boys! And we're going after the Germans who have holed up in the Alps!"

Everyone went wild. There was clapping and cheering and

hooting and hollering. Wiley leaped from his bunk and swung Cam around, sending Cam to the head once more and making everyone laugh. Only Noah and his uncle stayed silent. And Noah wondered just what going after the Germans atop those Alps would mean to them both.

CHAPTER TWENTY-SIX

The loudspeaker on the boat was playing Bing Crosby's "I'll Be Home for Christmas" when they entered the harbor at Naples, just two days before the holiday. The irony was not lost on Noah.

Wiley, Bill, Cam, Roger, and he had rushed to the deck when they first called out "land." It had taken twelve days to cross the Atlantic, and each of them was ready to step back on solid ground. Noah was also anxious to get a glimpse of Italy. He had heard it was a beautiful country, with large stretches of olive trees, taverns where music poured out, and museums filled with great works of art. As they approached, Noah could see Mount Vesuvius looming in the distance. He knew that the volcano was still active and that it had once blown and buried the city of Pompeii. Now it just looked peaceful and lovely, rising majestically over Naples.

As they came into the harbor, Wiley let out a loud whistle.

The water was littered with sunken ships and the remains of destroyed bridges. Their boat had to navigate its way slowly through the port to avoid colliding with all the debris. Oil floated on the clear blue Mediterranean waters.

"Those Germans!" Roger spat out angrily.

"The Germans didn't do this," James Shelley said, coming up beside them. "We did."

"Whatever for?" Bill asked.

"To get the Nazis *out*," Noah's uncle responded.

Noah stared around at the destruction. Was the fighting worth all this?

Noah and the boys followed his uncle and Skeeter off the ship when they reached the dock. Noah looked about him with wide-eyed wonder. The streets of Naples were the narrowest he had ever seen. They wound their way up from the harbor, light barely filtering its way between the four-story stone buildings. All around him, old men sat on benches talking to one another while old women leaned their elbows on their windowsills, shutters opened wide, and admonished them in Italian. Two-wheel horse-drawn carts vied with a few cars on the cobblestoned streets. A stone fountain in the middle of one of the squares sent up sprays of water. Girls walked by carrying large bundles of firewood and buckets of water, eyeing the soldiers. Several of the boys whistled at the girls, but Skeeter quickly silenced them with a look.

When they reached the center of the city, they were told to set their things down and wait. Noah stayed with Wiley, Olaf, and Bill while Skeeter, Daniel, and his uncle went on ahead with the general into a building, which Skeeter said housed the American and British headquarters in Naples.

Noah threw his pack down and sat next to it, leaning against Wiley.

"Let's see," Bill said, opening a book on Italian. "*Grazie.* That's Italian for thank you."

"*Grazie,*" Noah repeated.

"*Buongiorno,*" said Bill. "That means good day."

"*Buongiorno,*" Noah repeated. He liked learning Italian.

"Gee," Wiley said. "These Italians have a word for everything, don't they?"

"What'd you expect, you idiot?" Bill asked.

Everyone laughed.

Two little girls ran up to the boys and stood staring at them. The girls were barefoot, even in the bitter cold of the December morning. They had a raw, hungry look to them.

Bill handed the girls an open can of beans from his rucksack. Within seconds, the two girls had devoured the food.

"Jeesh," Cam whistled. "They sure are some hungry ones."

"They are all hungry," Olaf said to Noah and the other boys. "They are starving. The Germans have taken every bit of food from their mouths in order to feed their troops. It vas the same for us Norvegians just before I escaped.

"Look at the streets," he continued. "Before the var, these streets vould be filled vith vendors in open markets selling all kinds of food. Now everyone just hopes to stay alive."

Noah wondered how carts piled with food could even fit into these cobblestone streets.

"*Heil* Hitler!" Wiley made a mock salute.

The two girls still stood beside them, watching them with big brown eyes. They couldn't have been more than seven years of age.

"*Buongiorno*," Noah said to them.

"Hi, GI," one of the girls spoke up.

Everyone laughed again. Noah reached into his sack and pulled out a candy bar. He handed it to them and watched them split it in two and each eat their portion.

Quickly, the other boys began getting to their feet. Noah's uncle, Skeeter, Daniel, and the general had returned.

"Okay, men," James Shelley said. "Pick up your things. We've got our orders. We're heading north. The trucks leave in an hour."

"What's our assignment?" Bill asked.

"We'll be taking the trucks to Bagnoli and from there, a train to the Alps," James Shelley explained. "The army wants us to push the Germans off the top of those mountains and back through the Po Valley. That valley is important."

"Why?" Bill asked.

"It's one of the few places that is still fertile enough to provide food for the German army," the general said. "If we can get those Germans pushed out of there, their food supply will be cut off."

Suddenly, there was the sound of screaming and wailing from up one of the alleyways. Two men with a stretcher between them were running down the uneven cobblestones, weaving back and forth. On the stretcher lay a man, moaning and groaning.

They ran past Noah, and he could see that the man's legs were horribly twisted and that there was blood coming from his nose.

Behind the men came a woman dressed all in black, crying and wailing and holding her hands to her head.

"What the . . . ," Wiley began.

"Another partisan," Daniel explained. "Italian freedom fighters. They risk their lives getting information about the Germans for our men. When German Field Marshal Kesselring catches them, he tortures them for days. Then he leaves them out in the snow among the mines so more partisans are blown up trying to rescue their comrade."

Noah watched the man being carried down the street toward the hospital, his stomach churning.

"Welcome to war, Noah boy," his uncle said.

CHAPTER TWENTY-SEVEN

Snow and ice lay heavy across the hillsides and Alps of Italy. Olive trees sprinkled the countryside, their branches bare in winter. Noah could see the red tile roofs of the mountain village as they approached the small town where they would stay. Vidiciatico was near the top of the Italian "boot." Noah had found it on a map about halfway between Bologna and Florence.

As Noah stepped down from the train and swung his rucksack over his shoulder, he was surprised to find the local people awaiting their arrival. They smiled and waved as the Tenth Mountain Division marched along the road toward town. Noah smiled back. If he was going to war, it was nice to know that someone seemed grateful for his efforts.

In the village of Vidiciatico, they were divided up and sent to separate quarters to be housed. Noah, Wiley, Bill, Cam, and Roger were given space in the barn attached to a stone farmhouse. One tired old cow resided with them. Noah was thrilled with his bunkmates, both the boys and the animal, going over immediately to the cow and patting her thick sides. Cam was not as enamored.

"It smells like manure in here," he complained, setting his rucksack down on the barn floor.

"Give it a week," Noah told him. "I don't think we'll be showering on a regular basis, so soon you won't even know the difference between yourself and the cow."

"Smelling you, I can't tell the difference *now*," Wiley joked as he set down his things.

Cam kicked some of the hay at Wiley, and Wiley grinned as the straw floated feebly to the ground.

Bill went to the door of the barn and stood looking out. "It's kind of spooky, isn't it? Knowing they're up there, just waiting for us."

Noah shivered at Bill's words. Even from inside the barn, he could see the mountains on which the Germans were now ensconced: Mount Belvedere and Riva Ridge, one sharp and ragged-toothed and impossible-looking to climb, the other gentle and sloping with no protection for anyone trying to attack it. The Tenth Mountain Division had their job cut out for them if they were to be successful in pushing the enemy off their perch.

Suddenly, a voice cut through the quiet of the village. "Welcome, men of the Tenth Mountain Division!"

"Where the heck is that coming from?" Noah asked, going to the door with the others.

"You have come a long way from Camp Hale, Colorado," continued the voice in slightly accented English, floating down from the mountaintop.

"It's coming from up there!" Wiley cried, pointing. "It's the Germans!"

Other Tenth Mountain Division soldiers were appearing in doorways and coming out of alleys.

"How the heck do they know we're here?" Bill said.

"Worse," Cam whispered, his face white, "how do they know where we came from?"

"There's an old Italian expression, my friends," the voice boomed out on the loudspeaker, making Noah jump. "'See Naples and die.'"

There was a pause. "*You* have seen Naples." Then the world went silent again except for the shuffling of the cow in the barn behind them.

"I guess this is for real," Roger said.

Noah's stomach flipped, but whether from Roger's words or the German's, he wasn't sure.

"Scusa."

Noah turned at the sound of the lilting voice. He had just finished choosing a spot for himself, laying out his bedroll and emptying his rucksack, trying to create some kind of comfortable, homey-type space in the cold wooden barn. The words the Germans had sent their way had replayed over and over in his head as he went about laying out his gear, making the barn seem even colder than it was.

At the door stood a young girl, her dark hair held back with a head scarf, her skin clear and smooth, her large eyes framed with thick lashes. When she smiled boldly at them, Noah's breath caught with pleasure. All the boys jumped to their feet.

"*Mi chiamo Sofia,*" she said. "My name is Sofia. *Per favore.* Come with me."

"Sure! You bet!" Roger said, grinning, glancing back at his buddies and winking.

They followed Sofia to the farmhouse, where they had to duck to avoid hitting their heads on the low door frame as they entered. Inside the cottage, a fire burned in the large stone fireplace. Carved chairs surrounded a long wooden table. Kettles and pots hung from the wooden rafters overhead. Olaf and Noah's uncle sat by the fire with a man wrapped in thick blankets, talking in low voices. James Shelley looked up as the boys entered.

"Take a seat, gentlemen," he said. "Our hosts have been kind enough to prepare us a good meal."

Eagerly, Noah sat down with the others. Since they had left the boat, he'd been living on K-rations, cold beans, and canned meat. He licked his lips as he saw Sofia and her mother dipping a ladle into a large pot and dishing out hot soup and slicing fresh bread.

"*Grazie,*" Noah said, when Sofia came by to fill his bowl. She smiled warmly at him, and Noah's heart skipped a beat. But a moment later, he saw her smile at Bill and Roger, too.

James Shelley came to the table to join them. Sofia's mother poured some soup into his bowl. "*Grazie,*" Noah's uncle said.

Sofia's mother inclined her head in acknowledgment and then went to fill Olaf's bowl.

"Eat up now," James Shelley said. "The Germans have taken most everything around here for themselves. This feast being provided us is most generous of these people, and we don't want to appear ungrateful."

Noah saw that Sofia was still standing, as was her mother.

"Would you like to sit down?" he asked, scooting closer to Wiley and making space beside him.

She shook her head. *"No, prego."* She motioned with her hand to show that she meant the boys to eat, that she was there to serve.

"Noah?"

Noah forced his eyes from the girl to find his uncle giving him an amused look.

"You do remember why we're here, don't you?"

"How could we forget?" Wiley said, as he bit off a chunk of bread. "Those Germans sure were keen on *reminding* us this afternoon."

"Yeah," Cam complained. "How do they know all about us? That's creepy."

"That's vhat spies are for," Olaf said, taking a sip of soup. "But do not vorry. Ve have spies of our own." He nodded toward where the old man sat by the fire.

"Sofia's grandfather is a spy?" Noah asked.

"That is *mio padre*," Sofia spoke up.

Noah looked over at the man in surprise. He had hardly

moved from where he sat, blankets covering his legs. This was Sofia's father? He seemed ancient.

"Why isn't he out fighting?" Roger asked.

"He was hurt," Sofia answered, in heavily accented English. "He is a partisan and was caught by Germans. *Padre*," she called to him. She spoke rapidly in Italian.

The man by the fire lifted his blanket up. He was missing his legs.

"Papa was caught and the bones of his legs were smashed with a hammer by the Germans," Sofia said. "When we finally got to him, it was too late to save his legs."

Noah's spoon halted halfway to his mouth.

"But *mio padre*," she continued, her eyes gleaming with pride, "he still remembered some valuable information even though he had been tortured. Because of him, we were able to destroy an incoming trainload of German soldiers."

Noah set his spoon down abruptly, horrified at the atrocity that had been committed upon her father and the fact that Sofia was actually proud of blowing up a train. She caught his glance.

"It is us or them, GI," she reminded him scornfully, "and legs are a small price to pay for freedom."

CHAPTER TWENTY-EIGHT

The days began to fall into a pattern. Noah woke early, rising to help Sofia with the milking of the cow, the only one left in Vidiciatico that the Germans hadn't found and taken. When the milking was finished, Sofia and he carefully divided the precious liquid into smaller containers and delivered them to other houses in the village, sharing the bulk of the milk with families who had small children. When they returned, Cam, Roger, Bill, and Wiley would be up and ready to help Sofia with her other chores.

Noah was grateful that the others were too lazy to rise as early as he did. He welcomed his time with Sofia. Though she never encouraged him and spoke only occasionally, there was something soothing about doing farm work with her by his side. It reminded him of home. As if life, in spite of the war, would go on. And, too, it helped ease his fears about the upcoming evenings.

The entire Tenth Mountain Division had been divided into groups for night patrolling. Noah, Wiley, and Daniel were led out by Skeeter every other night. Cam, Roger, and Bill took the opposite nights with Noah's uncle. Olaf was instructed to work with the local partisans, as his experience as a Norwegian freedom fighter would be of value to these men and women who fought secretly against the Germans.

Noah dressed warmly when it was his night for scouting. Sometimes his hands shook as he zipped up his parka or tied up his ski boots.

He would join Wiley and Daniel to be briefed by Skeeter before they set out.

"We've got to find several ways up Riva," Skeeter said to them, pointing to a map that lay on the table. "If we can get up there and wrest it from the Germans, they won't be able to defend Belvedere as well. We'll have taken a high point from them. If they keep Riva, our boys will be sitting ducks for them as they attempt Belvedere. The Germans will just be able to shoot them off, one by one, from that vantage point. Before we climb and attempt to take Riva, we'll need to do a little reconnaissance work.

"Here are some of the questions we need to answer before we can attack," Skeeter continued. "What is the terrain like? Wiley, I'm ordering you to carry a map to make notes as we patrol. How has the enemy moved? If we run into their communication lines, can we cut them?"

"Won't they notice?" Wiley asked.

Skeeter grinned. "We won't cut them now, Wiley. We'll cut them the night we attack Riva."

Wiley turned as red as his hair, and Noah gave a small laugh. It settled him and gave him a small jolt of courage.

"Remember to look for footprints in the snow," Daniel warned them.

Noah looked at him, puzzled.

"Footprints," Daniel repeated. "Think, Garrett. If you see footprints that means some German has been sneaking down near our camp, maybe spying on us, maybe even putting a man in our midst."

Noah hadn't thought of that. It was bad enough sneaking about in the night, hoping the Germans up on the ridge didn't spot you and start firing. It was worse to know that they would be walking around in the night, too, spying on you just as you were spying on them.

"We have a password," Skeeter said, "and it will change every night. Remember it. Should you run into someone else out there, use it. If they don't know it, the soldier won't be one of ours."

Noah knew what that meant. If he wasn't one of ours, he was one of theirs.

That first night, Noah's mouth was dry as they stepped out into the darkness. He skied right behind Daniel, trying to keep pace and not be left behind. Their skis made swishing noises in the packed snow, noises that sounded as loud as a brass band to Noah's ears.

Moving like ghosts, they flitted in among the trees to the bottom of Riva and began to search for ways to get up the steep slope. Noah watched every little movement around him, his heart jumping when the trees swayed with the night wind, when snow swirled up suddenly in a mist, when the moon changed the patterns of the shadows on the ground.

Skeeter had told them that the Germans, too, were camouflaged. Just because you wore white didn't mean you were friendly. If they ran into the enemy, they were to try and take them alive so they could be questioned. Noah didn't need to be told that the reverse was also true. The Germans would be looking for a Tenth Mountain Division soldier to interrogate. And Noah thought of Sofia's father and the Germans' interrogation techniques.

Every night, they made their way farther up the mountain, mapping various ways to climb and attack the ridge. Every night, when Noah made it safely back, he undid his skis and slid off his rucksack and gun, grateful he hadn't run into trouble. But sometimes at night, he'd wake from a nightmare and lie staring up at the ceiling of the barn, waiting for daylight and Sofia's light step and the sound of her tin pails hitting softly against each other to ease his racing thoughts.

December melted into January. One evening right before patrols, Bill came down with a fever and chills. Noah helped his uncle carry Bill to the makeshift hospital that had been set up in the town hall.

"He'll be fine," the doctor told them, "but he'll have to stay here for a few nights."

"I can go with you instead," Noah volunteered, though the idea of going out three nights in a row scared him to death.

"No," James Shelley said. "It's bad enough the general wouldn't assign you to my patrol, though he's right that I'd probably be so concerned for your safety, I'd stop paying attention to everyone else's. I'll take Skeeter with me tonight, and then we'll see what we can do until Bill recovers."

Noah nodded his agreement and walked back to the farmhouse with his uncle.

"Good luck," he said to his uncle as he turned toward the barn and a card game with Wiley.

His uncle nodded and moved off to inform the general and Skeeter about Bill's condition.

That night, Noah woke with an uneasy feeling. He heard the sound of shooting in the distance. As his eyes adjusted to the dark of the barn, he could see the outline of someone sitting on the milking stool not far from him. Quietly, he turned his head toward Wiley. He could just make out his lumpy shape a few feet away. Roger and Cam were on patrol with his uncle and Skeeter. Bill was in the hospital. Olaf and Daniel had been staying in the farmhouse along with his uncle and Skeeter. So who was sitting there, barely moving?

Noah's heart pounded loudly in his ears as he silently inched his hand toward his gun. He removed the safety. The click of it was loud in the darkness of the barn. The figure turned toward him.

"Put it away!"

Slowly, Noah replaced the safety and sat up, relief flooding through him at the sound of his uncle's voice.

"What are you doing here?" Noah asked. "What's wrong?"

James Shelley didn't answer.

Noah got out of his sleeping bag, shivering in the cold. He grabbed a blanket and wrapped it around him and went over to his uncle, who stared up at him with unseeing eyes. The cow shuffled around in the hay of her stall.

"Shelley?" Noah asked. "What is it?"

His uncle finally focused on Noah. "It's Skeeter. He tripped a wire."

"No," Noah said, the breath rushing out of him, thinking of how carefully last night they had skirted the mines and trip wires the Germans had set as traps for the Tenth Mountain Division. Had Skeeter been too tired to go out tonight?

"He may not make it," his uncle added.

Noah sat down heavily as his uncle's words sank in.

"I brought him back myself, and they're operating on him now," his uncle said. "He fell forward onto the mine and was torn right up the middle. It split him apart. The Germans heard the explosion and started shooting. We all got separated. I'm hoping Cam and Roger make it back in one piece."

"Cam and Roger might be hurt, too?" Noah asked.

"Could be," his uncle said. "We'll just have to wait and see."

"How can you be so calm about this?" Noah said, his voice rising as he thought about Skeeter and Roger and Cam. "How can you talk about this so rationally?"

His uncle rose from the stool and sighed. "I just can't think about it, Noah. It hurts too much."

"So?" Noah said. "It's supposed to hurt, Shelley."

"Hey, what's going on?" Wiley asked, sitting up, wide awake now.

His uncle ignored Wiley. "Noah, you live your life with your feelings on the surface. Why, if it was possible, I could reach out my hand and touch them every day. But me, well, I've lived a lot of years now with it all inside. I can't afford to think about Skeeter right now. I just can't."

His uncle walked toward the barn door.

Noah watched him go, thinking about the callousness his uncle had shown him when they first met, how he'd thrown the door into the bunkhouse upon learning how his sister had died, how he was gruff and distant on one level and yet still cared deeply about Noah on another.

And he thought of Skeeter and his comments that night back at Camp Hale, his statement that life wasn't black and white, that nothing was that simple. Noah went to the barn door. In the moonlight, he could just see his uncle walking across the yard toward the old stone house.

"Uncle Shelley," Noah called out.

His uncle turned.

"I'm sorry," Noah said.

"Forget it," he said. "It's nothing. Get yourself dressed, Noah. When I'm done, I'll take you to see Skeeter. I know that's what *you* need."

CHAPTER TWENTY-NINE

Cam and Roger were at the hospital when Wiley, Noah, and his uncle arrived. Roger had taken a bullet to his shoulder, and Cam was beside him, his face white.

"Glad to see you boys made it back safely," James Shelley said.

"Wouldn't have if Cam hadn't picked me up and carried me here," Roger said, his eyes squeezing tight in pain as the doctor probed the wound.

Cam was hopping nervously from foot to foot. "It was wild out there, wasn't it, Shelley? Wasn't it? It was, wasn't it?"

Noah looked over at his uncle, unsure how to react to Cam's strange behavior.

Wiley went and put his arm around Cam. "Hey, buddy, what do you say you and me go do a little celebrating? You're a hero, you know."

"Celebrate? Yeah, that's the ticket," Cam said. "We should go celebrate. Right, Shelley? We should all celebrate!"

Wiley nodded to Noah's uncle, who nodded back. He led Cam away, down the corridor and out of the hospital.

"What's the matter with him?" Noah asked.

"Shock," Roger replied, as the doctor wiped his hands on a towel. "Wiley and I both saw it when we were at Kiska. I sure hope Cam bounces out of it."

"You and me both," James Shelley agreed.

"You mean he might not?" Noah asked, thinking of the picture of Cam and his little brother with the missing front teeth and how his little brother had seen Cam as a hero.

His uncle shrugged. "War does funny things to people, Noah. And not just physically, either."

He turned to the doctor who was looking at Roger's shoulder. "And how about him? Is he gonna be all right?"

The doctor nodded. "Seems like the bullet went right through. I'll sew him up, and he'll be ready to go."

"Can't keep me down, Shelley," Roger said, grinning. "I owe them Germans one."

"And Skeeter?" Noah asked, his voice cracking a bit.

The doctor shook his head. "They're operating on him now. But it doesn't look good."

"Jeesh, we're losing boys fast. And we haven't even officially *attacked* yet!" The general had walked up behind them. He went over to Roger. "How you doing there, soldier?"

"I'll be fine, General," Roger said.

"Good to hear," the general said. "Well then, it looks like we've got some waiting to do." He sat down and leaned back in his chair. "It's going to be a long night, fellas."

Around four A.M., a doctor operating on Skeeter came out, wiping sweat from his brow with the back of his arm. Noah had been dozing, but he leaped to his feet when he heard the operating room doors open and close. James Shelley was standing, leaning against one wall. The general rose from his chair. Daniel Stultz had slipped in at one point during the night and was standing next to the outside door.

"How is he?" the general asked.

"Can't say for sure yet," the doctor said. "It's still touch and go. Either way, he won't be ready for the assault."

Daniel Stultz swore softly under his breath.

"Seems to me we should just be worried he'll make it at all," Noah said pointedly to Daniel.

Daniel ignored him. "We'll have to reconfigure the attack, sir. Without Skeeter to lead, we'll need to move someone else up."

The general nodded wearily. "In the morning, Daniel, in the morning. Right now, let's all go get some sleep. Skeeter's alive. Let's be thankful for that."

Just then, the doors to the operating room opened again, and they wheeled Skeeter out. He was bandaged tightly. His lips were bloodless and his face pale. Noah watched him go, looking at the price of war.

Sun poured in through the cracks of the old barn door, waking Noah. He shivered in the cold morning air and pulled the blankets tighter around him. Then he remembered Skeeter, and his heart sank. He wished he could close his eyes again and forget this nightmare. He wished he could wave his hand and have them all safely back at Camp Hale.

Beside him, Wiley turned over and slowly sat up. He said nothing, just stared out unseeingly at the light in the barn.

Noah broke the silence. "How's Cam?"

Wiley shrugged. "Having his head examined today. Hope he hasn't totally lost it. Skeeter?"

Noah sat up and shrugged, too. "Too early to tell."

Wiley pushed back his covers and went to the barn door, pushing it open. Snow had fallen the night before, covering the mountains and countryside in a thick layer of white. Noah caught his breath. It was beautiful, and the incongruity of the horror last night and the magnificence of this morning shocked him.

Wiley turned. "How about a little fun?"

Noah nodded. Whatever Wiley's idea was, it had to be better than sitting here thinking about Skeeter and Cam.

The air was crisp and clear as Wiley and Noah headed out, away from Riva and Belvedere and the small town of Vidiciatico. Their skis slid easily over the newly fallen snow. It felt good to push out hard and fast, and Noah felt the sweat building and his muscles responding to the quick pace. They climbed one hill and skied down the other side, moving farther and farther away from their base camp and the reminders of last night. Still, they could not escape the signs of war.

Houses stood with roofs missing. Barns were collapsed on themselves, bombed so badly they were no longer of any use. The people they passed looked weary and hungry, their clothes so threadbare they barely covered them. Still, they managed a wave and a tired smile after their initial fear at the two soldiers skiing past them. When the villagers realized they were Americans, they trudged on, seeing to their chores around the quiet farmland of their country.

Noah pushed the memory of Skeeter on the gurney to the back of his mind. He followed Wiley up one slope and down another, enjoying the thrill of speed and the beauty of turns well made. Wiley hooted and hollered with each fast-paced descent.

As they crested one hill, Noah stopped with Wiley and looked out over the valley below. The area was circled by mountains and surrounded by thick stands of trees. The sun shone brightly, lighting patches of snow caught between branches. A small group of stone buildings clustered close to one patch of trees. Noah took in the beauty of Italy. This far from Vidiciatico, the world seemed at peace.

"This was a great idea, Wiley," Noah said. "I feel better already."

Wiley nodded his agreement.

The door to one of the low stone buildings swung open, and from the hillside, Noah saw Sofia step out. He drew in his breath in surprise. "What's she doing here? We're miles from Vidiciatico."

"Maybe she's visiting someone," Wiley said.

"But there's nothing around," Noah argued. "No cart or horse. It's too long a walk."

Below them, Sofia pulled a set of skis from against the building and threw them to the ground. Noah laughed. "I can't believe I thought we were the only skiers around here!"

Wiley grinned at him. "Hey. Let's go surprise her."

Together, they took off down the hill, skiing fast and hard. As they drew near, Sofia looked up, fear crossing her face.

"Sofia!" Noah called out.

With the sound of his voice came a quick *POP!* Then another *POP!*

"For God's sake," Sofia shouted, ducking her head and quickly attaching the skis to her boots. "Get out of here!"

She waved them back.

"It's Germans!" Wiley shouted to Noah. "They're shooting from the opposite hillside."

Noah didn't need to be told twice. He turned and headed back the way they'd come. As he was scrambling to turn his skis, he saw the door open again, and Olaf poked his head out.

"Vhat the heck?" he called to Sofia.

"*Abbiamo un problema*," Sofia called to Olaf. "We've been discovered."

Noah didn't wait to hear what had been found out. He took off, Wiley and Sofia right behind him.

POP! POP! POP!

Noah's arms shook as he duck-walked his way back up the hill, digging his poles into the snow to get as much distance as he could. Sofia soon overtook him, moving at a pace Noah found amazing.

"You fools!" she hissed as she flew by them. "You led those Germans right to us!"

They crested the hill. Noah turned. Behind him came Olaf and two others, a man and a woman.

"*Rapido!*" Sofia cried. "They must not catch us."

Noah followed her lead and sped down the side of the mountain, watching as Sofia glided from side to side with an ease that eluded him. Soon Olaf, the man and woman, and Wiley were passing him by.

"Quickly, Noah," Olaf commanded, slowing down to help Noah along.

POP! POP! POP!

Noah turned and saw white figures cresting the hill behind him.

"Do not stop!" Olaf called.

Noah didn't need any further encouragement. He scurried up the next hill and sped down the other side. Up the next, down the next, over and over until at last everyone came to a stop and turned to look back. The hill behind them remained bare.

"Vhat vere you doing there?" Olaf yelled at him.

Noah felt himself redden.

"We just went out for a ski," Wiley explained. "We just needed a little fun."

"Did you clear this vith your uncle, Noah?" Olaf asked.

Noah shook his head in embarrassment.

"You almost got us and yourselves killed or captured," Sofia cried.

"But what are you doing out there?" Noah asked. "And why were the Germans following us?"

"Ve vere meeting our partisan contacts at vhat ve thought vas a safe house," Olaf said angrily.

"The Germans followed you from camp, probably hoping to capture you or kill you. Now our safe house is no longer safe," Sofia spat out. "Nor are these people of any use to us as spies. They've been seen."

The man and woman stood looking worriedly behind them, obviously not understanding much English.

"I'm sorry," Noah said. "We just needed a little relaxation. It's been hard this week with Skeeter getting hurt, Roger getting shot, and Cam losing his mind."

"*Per te?*" Sofia said scornfully. "It has been hard for *you* this *week*? Perhaps, my friend, you should remember that for us Italians, it has been hard for years. Then you might think a little longer before you do something this foolish."

Noah didn't know what to say. Sofia was right.

"There is nothing for it now," Olaf said. "Ve must head back."

Noah followed them back to Vidiciatico, feeling stupid and ashamed.

CHAPTER THIRTY

Sofia wouldn't talk to Noah for days afterward. Even when he got up early and began their chores long before she opened the barn door, she remained mute and angry.

Noah knew she had a right to her anger. Her father had given his legs for freedom. And now Noah had placed others like him and their cause in jeopardy.

"Don't know why you keep trying to get her to talk," Wiley grumbled.

"I feel bad," Noah said.

"We didn't mean to do it," Wiley argued. "We were just having a little fun. Considering how we spend our nights, going for a ski doesn't seem all that horrible."

Wiley had been arguing this point of view since they got back, when they were given a good dressing-down by Noah's uncle. But Wiley had always been gung ho about the war. His feelings were less ambivalent and so, Noah reasoned, he felt less guilt.

Wiley knew he was giving 100 percent of himself to the cause. For Noah, it was less clear.

The snow that had fallen so quickly the night before their ski trip melted just as swiftly. Noah found himself walking through thick mud as he made his way to the hospital to visit Skeeter.

His uncle was sitting by Skeeter's bedside.

"How is he?" Noah whispered.

"Sleeping," James Shelley answered, "but not well. He's moaning a bit. Do you mind going and fetching the doctor?"

Noah did as his uncle asked.

The doctor came quickly, examining Skeeter for a minute and then straightening up. "I think we'd better increase his dosage of morphine. The longer he rests, the quicker his body will heal and the less pain he'll be in. I don't want him coming fully into consciousness just yet."

He glanced around the ward. "I need help here to turn him on his side."

"I can help," Noah volunteered.

The doctor looked for a minute at Noah. "All right. But you must be careful."

Noah nodded. He did as the doctor directed him, being sure not to jostle Skeeter too much or make any quick movements that might cause him more pain.

"Hold him there, if you don't mind," the doctor said.

He filled a needle with morphine and gave Skeeter the shot to ease him back into sleep. Skeeter moaned slightly but did not come fully awake.

When they finally had Skeeter on his back and resting

comfortably, Noah turned to see his uncle staring at him. "You did that good, boy."

Noah shrugged.

The doctor patted Noah on the shoulder. "I could use about ten more like him in this ward."

A nurse came calling for the doctor, and he left Noah alone with his uncle and Skeeter.

Bill came walking up. "Hey, Noah. Hey, Shelley."

"You feeling better, boy?" Noah's uncle asked.

Bill nodded. "Fever's gone, so I guess I'm ready to report back to duty, sir."

"That's a good thing," Noah's uncle said. "Now that we've lost Skeeter and Cam, we need you. With this snow melting fast during the day and the temperature dropping at night, we're facing ice."

Noah knew slick conditions would make the reconnaissance work even more dangerous than before. His heart skipped a beat remembering that tonight was his night to patrol again.

"We're counting down, boys. It's only a matter of days now. The more knowledge of those mountains we get before we attack, the more chance we'll have of succeeding," his uncle said grimly. "And we can't fail. For Skeeter and all the others like him, we just can't fail."

That night, Noah walked stealthily away from town, moving as silently and swiftly as he could. In the mud and muck, their skis were no longer of any use. Noah's heart pounded with each step into the darkness. Having been shot at, he was now well aware of the risk he took and just how close the Germans were willing to get to obtain their own information, too.

"Careful of mines and trip wires," Daniel whispered back to Noah and Wiley. "Stay alert."

As if either of them *needed* reminding. They only had to stop by Skeeter's bedside to remember what resulted from not concentrating fully.

Noah trained his eyes on the mud, straining to see if there were any signs of the ground having been tampered with. Wiley carried the map. Daniel and Noah did the scouting, silently pointing out the tough spots for Wiley to note as they made their way up the ridge.

They had just reached a mountain stream when Daniel, who had gone ahead a bit, came hurrying back to them. He motioned them toward the trees that bordered the water, mouthing "Germans" as he slipped away into the darkness.

Noah's mouth went dry. Quickly, he followed Wiley to a stand of trees and pulled his rifle from his rucksack, propping the bag down at his feet against the tree. He turned to look at Wiley, whose face was white in the blackness of the night. Wiley gave him a thumbs-up sign, grinned, and stepped behind another tree until Noah could no longer see him.

It was then that he heard voices, German voices. Noah pushed his back up against the hard wooden trunk. The uneven bark poked him, but he didn't move. He tried to still his breathing, afraid that even that sound might give him away. The voices came closer. Noah could feel the blood coursing through his veins in hot, fast throbs.

The voices moved even closer and then, slowly, faded away. Noah let out a sigh of relief.

Suddenly, a loud shot disrupted the quiet of the moment. Noah jumped. A few feet away, a German stepped out from the very tree Wiley had gone to hide behind.

Noah wanted to cry for help, but before he could open his mouth, a hand was pushed against it. Noah struggled against his captor, pushing and pulling to wrench himself free.

"For God's sake, hold still!" Daniel's voice hissed in Noah's ear.

Noah went slack, and Daniel dropped his hand from Noah's mouth. The two of them watched the German turn and walk swiftly away to join the others in his group. Noah heard laughter from a distance. His whole body shook as he held himself still and waited impatiently for the Germans to be gone. Then he could stand it no longer. Without consulting Daniel, he broke away and ran across the ground between him and Wiley.

Behind the tree, Wiley lay in a pool of blood. Noah bit hard down on his lip to stop from screaming out into the night and alerting the Germans that they were still there.

Daniel stepped up beside him. "I'm sorry, Noah."

Noah kept shaking his head back and forth. "No, no, no, no, no," he whispered over and over to himself. It didn't matter how many times he said it, though. Noah knew the truth. Wiley, the very first of his friends, was dead.

CHAPTER THIRTY-ONE

Noah?" James Shelley sat down on the barn floor. "I know it doesn't mean much for me to say this, but I'm sorry, boy."

Noah just lay there, staring up at the rafters of the barn. He'd lain like that since he and Daniel had returned three days ago, not responding to anyone when they tried to talk to him.

He kept reliving the horror of having to carry Wiley back here, Wiley's head lolling to one side, his red hair drooping into his unseeing eyes, his chest sticky with blood. Daniel had tried to convince Noah to come back for Wiley later, when the woods would be empty of Germans on patrol. But Noah had refused to leave Wiley there. He'd bent down to pick Wiley up and carry him home, and Daniel had complied by lending a hand. And not until Noah had gently laid Wiley on a clean white sheet at the hospital had he finally given in to his own pain. Then it was Daniel who had picked Noah up from where he had slumped to the floor and brought him to the barn.

"Noah," his uncle continued, "please don't tell me I've lost you in the clouds somewhere like Cam. Come on, boy. Speak to me. Let it out."

Noah could hear the pain in his uncle's voice. He wanted to say something, but he couldn't. The hurt was too great.

His uncle bent over him. "Noah. Let me in. Let me help you." His uncle's voice cracked. "Please don't leave me to believe that I've messed this all up."

"*Basta!*"

Sofia's voice was loud in the barn.

"Stop lying about like some beaten-up old dog!" she commanded, now standing above Noah, staring down at him.

"What are you thinking, girl," James Shelley snapped, "speaking in that tone to my nephew? Do you not get it? Noah and Wiley were friends."

"Not get it?" Sofia laughed, turning on Noah's uncle. "*Mio padre* has no legs, and my grandmother was shot by the Wehrmacht last winter in retaliation for another German being shot. What exactly do you think I don't get?"

Noah turned his eyes to watch her. His mind began to drift from the woods and focus on her angry face.

"We've all been through a lot, Sofia," James Shelley said. "We all just handle loss differently."

"By sulking?" Sofia asked, a smirk on her face. "By curling up and giving up? No disrespect meant here, *signore*, but if we all did that, we'd be speaking German right about now."

"That's enough!" James Shelley said. "I'll not have another word from you about my nephew. Leave him be."

"I can defend myself, Shelley," Noah whispered.

"How about getting up and defending others, then?" Sofia challenged him. "Or maybe you'd prefer to wallow here in the barn until you feel better?"

"Sofia!" Noah's uncle bellowed. He rose and pointed to the door. "Out!"

Noah sat up. "Wait!"

His uncle turned and looked at him questioningly.

"Leave us for a minute, would you, Shelley?" Noah asked.

"She shouldn't be talking to you like this, Noah," his uncle said. "We're here defending her country. She has no right."

"She has every right, Shelley." Noah sighed. "She's had every right since the day freedom was taken from her." He looked up at his uncle. "Go on. I'll be fine."

His uncle hesitated, then nodded. At the door, he turned. "If I hear any shouting from you," he said, pointing a finger at Sofia, "I'll be back here with a muzzle to shut you up. Understand?"

When James Shelley had left, Sofia pulled out a milking stool and sat down. "All right, GI. Why don't you tell me about Wiley?"

Noah's eyes rested on hers like a drowning man's on a life preserver. To her, he would talk.

An hour later, Noah finished. He was exhausted, but all the stories of Wiley had been told, all the exploits, all the memories of his goofy face and red hair. He'd said everything there was to say, even describing Wiley's death and the look of him on that white sheet. She had listened, and he had wept.

Sofia came over to him and knelt down. "No one's ever really gone, Noah. They'll always be here."

Softly, she touched his chest, then she leaned in and kissed him lightly on the cheek.

Noah closed his eyes and let the feeling of life run through him.

"Now, GI," Sofia said, moving briskly away, the moment of intimacy over, "would you like some good news? Skeeter is sitting up. And they could use your help at the hospital. So let's get over there and get back to work."

She reached out her hand and Noah took it, letting her pull him to his feet and back into the war.

For the next few days, the general assigned Noah to hospital duty. Noah was grateful to his uncle, for he knew it had been his doing. He welcomed the respite from the night patrols and any situation that might have made him choose between killing or being killed.

Skeeter was awake, talking a bit, even smiling once in a while. He still had a lot of healing to do, and he was badly scarred. But he would live. Noah gave thanks every day he saw Skeeter grow a bit stronger.

Noah found his work in the hospital strangely rewarding. He stayed there long past his assigned hours. He ran errands for the nurses, changed bedpans, and read to Skeeter when he grew bored and restless. He wished he were trained to do more. He constantly asked questions about what the doctors were doing and asked them to show him what they could. It was fascinating to him.

Sofia met him there every day, sometimes bringing bread and cheese for lunch and sitting with him while he ate. They never talked about Wiley or that night again, but Noah was comforted knowing that he could if he wanted to.

One day, Sofia breezed in while Noah was trying to hear Skeeter's heart through the doctor's stethoscope. James Shelley sat by Skeeter's bedside.

"No, no," the doctor said, "move it a little lower." He pushed Skeeter's hospital gown aside.

"Hey! What do you think I am? Some kind of science experiment?" Skeeter mumbled.

"Right about there." The doctor took Noah's hand and moved the stethoscope down a bit. "Go ahead. Try now."

The room was quiet as Noah listened, awed at hearing the *pump, pump* of Skeeter's heart through his big chest.

"You should be a doctor someday, Noah," Sofia said as she came toward them.

James Shelley laughed. "Oh, that's a good one, girl. The boy can't even find Skeeter's heart properly!"

"I still say he'd make an excellent doctor," Sofia asserted.

Noah grinned at her, bending over the basket she carried. "All I want to doctor now is whatever you've brought me to eat."

"How about sharing a bit of the good stuff, Noah?" Skeeter begged.

"Hospital food only for you, soldier," the doctor commanded. "You chew on that rich food, and you won't live to fight another day. So eat your oatmeal and get your sleep."

Turning to Noah's uncle, Skeeter complained, "Hey, Shelley,

come on now. I helped you out when you were sick. How about a little assistance for me? Tell that rascal nephew of yours to start sharing the wealth."

But James Shelley didn't respond. He was lost in thought.

"Shelley?" Noah said, waving a hand in front of his uncle's face. "You okay?"

"Yeah, yeah," James Shelley responded. But without another word, he stood and walked away, and Noah was left wondering what was wrong with his uncle.

CHAPTER THIRTY-TWO

"Pack 'em up, boys. We're heading out." Noah's uncle stood in the doorway of the barn.

"Where're we going, Shelley?" Bill asked.

"Town by the name of Lucca, about sixty miles from here," he said. "And bring everything you have. We won't be coming back to the barn."

"What are we going for?" Roger asked.

"To refresh your climbing skills," Shelley answered.

Roger grinned with pleasure. Noah turned away. He didn't need to be told what this signified. Brushing up on training could only mean one thing. The assault on Riva and Belvedere was inching closer. Quietly, he rolled up his sleeping bag and began to pack his gear.

Before they left, he tried to find Sofia. But she was nowhere to be found. From the back of the truck, Noah watched the town of

Vidiciatico grow smaller and smaller. He wished he could have said good-bye to her.

The first few weeks of February had been unseasonably warm, and the town of Lucca was filled with muddy ruts as the Tenth Mountain Division made their way to the marble quarries on the outskirts of town. The truck bounced and jostled the boys riding in the back as they sang and Roger waved to the girls of the town, who stood along the side of the road to watch them pass.

Once at the quarry, though, they were put straight to work. For a few days, they were reminded of their time at Camp Hale as each of them rappelled down the sides of the high quarry walls and then scrambled back up them. In spite of his sore shoulder, Roger was ecstatic, pushing off and flying out on his descent with an enthusiasm that hadn't been seen in many weeks. Bill worked hard to improve his skills, asking questions and practicing over and over with a calmness and steadiness that Noah admired.

Noah wished he could capture some of Roger's excitement and Bill's strength. But every jump and every handhold reminded him of Wiley and of Cam, one dead and the other sent back stateside when he hadn't come out of the craziness that now clouded his head. Noah's heart went out to Cam's parents and his little brother, and he prayed that their presence again in his life would bring Cam back from the edge.

Noah felt as gloomy as Dour Dan Stultz. But for once, he understood Daniel's dedication and commitment. Working hard and practicing hard meant fewer mistakes and fewer lives lost when the time to attack finally came. Still, Noah was envious of

Roger and Bill, and he longed for the innocence of his first rappel with Olaf.

On February 17, they were ordered to pack their things again and prepare to hike out. The Tenth Mountain Division had been divided once more into their three infantry regiments of the 85th, 86th, and 87th for the attack. Several hours later and under cover of darkness, Noah and the boys of the 86th regiment slipped into the small towns that lay at the base of Riva Ridge not far from Vidiciatico. Groups of them were housed in various cottages and barns in the area.

Around midnight, Noah's uncle came to the cottage where Bill, Roger, and Noah were staying. Behind him were Daniel, Olaf, and the general. James Shelley did not look at Noah.

"Boys," the general said in a low voice, "tomorrow's the night. You three, along with the rest of the 86th, will be heading up Riva Ridge."

"At last," Roger crowed, "we're really going after those Germans!"

"So, how's it all going to work?" Bill asked.

Olaf spread out a map and used his finger to point out the way. "Bill and Roger, you vill go out vith Shelley and take this path up Riva, along vith about thirty others from the 86th. Shelley vill lead, and Roger, you vill be in the rear as you have practiced." He traced a path on the map. "Noah, you vill climb a few hundred yards away from them vith your group of thirty. Skeeter vill lead and Daniel vill bring up the rear just as in exercises. The rest of the boys vill be divided into other companies and encircle the mountain, each company taking a different vay up. I vill go with the 85th and 87th up Belvedere the next night. But ve can only take Belvedere if you are —"

"Skeeter?" Noah interrupted him. "Skeeter will *lead*? He can't make that climb!"

Noah turned to look at his uncle, and at last, Shelley met his gaze. Noah caught his breath at the misery he saw reflected there.

"Skeeter insists on coming along," the general told them. "I know he's not up to full strength yet, Noah, but we just don't have anyone else to lead your company up Riva Ridge. We need him. We have to have two leaders for each company, one out front, one behind."

"The climb up Riva could kill him," Bill blurted out.

"Yes, it could, but Skeeter knows that," Daniel spoke up. "And the success of this climb could save thousands of lives — Italian lives, British lives, other American lives."

"But it's Skeeter," Noah protested, turning to his uncle. "Can't you stop him from taking this chance? It's his life you're talking about."

Noah's uncle shook his head. "Skeeter wouldn't want it any other way. I'm sorry. Skeeter feels he can make the climb, and we've decided to let him go."

"Don't think it doesn't break our hearts to put such a good man like that at risk," the general said.

"Every man's going to be at risk that night, General," Daniel reminded him, "and every man who's willing to go and try is a good man."

The general sighed. "Of course, Daniel, of course. Still, when this war's over, I think I'm going to retire and open a bait and tackle shop."

"Aw, General," Noah's uncle said, grinning, "then you'll just be moaning about how unfair fishing is for the fish."

"You're probably right, Shelley," the general said, laughing. "You're probably right."

A year ago, Noah would have been angry about the way they were joking about something so serious. But he knew them all too well now. Joking was just their way of dealing with the fear.

The next day, Noah stood uncertainly outside the makeshift office that had been set up for the general. He looked at the closed door, feeling shaky inside. Quietly, he knocked.

"Who's there?" the general's voice boomed out.

"It's Noah Garrett, sir," Noah responded.

He entered the general's office. The general stood surrounded by maps.

"What is it, Noah?" the general asked. He looked impatient.

"Request permission to assume Skeeter's position for the assault, sir," Noah said.

The general looked up from his maps. He eyed Noah sharply. Then he laughed. "I can't do that, Noah. Your uncle would kill me, and I don't intend to be a casualty of war before we've even begun to fight."

"Begging your pardon, sir, but he doesn't need to know," Noah said.

The general's eyes narrowed. "What are you saying, Noah?"

Noah took a deep breath. "Skeeter can't make that climb, General. I've patrolled those mountains, too. I request permission to lead my company, sir."

The general stared at him. "Are you crazy? You're too young, and we're talking about war here, son. You didn't even want to join up in the first place."

"Actually, sir, I'm talking about Skeeter," Noah said. "You know he won't make it. Even if he survives the climb, he'll die afterward from exhaustion." Noah paused. "I admit I still don't know if war is right or wrong, General. But I . . . I . . . I want Skeeter to live. I want to do this for him."

"And if *you* should die being out front like that?" the general asked sternly. "What if tonight's climb puts you in the position of having to kill? What then, Noah?"

Noah shrugged. "If I have to save the lives of the boys behind me, then I'll do it, General. And I'll just remind myself of the lives I'm saving, not the lives I'm taking.

"I do know it's right to protect the ones you care about, no matter the cost," Noah said, though his voice wavered as he spoke. "Isn't that what this war is about?"

The general sighed. "I wish I knew, Noah. All I do know is that war's darn ugly."

Noah nodded.

The general remained silent for a minute. "What makes you so sure you can do Skeeter's job?"

"Because of all the times I patrolled with him," Noah said. "Look, General, I know I'm not Skeeter. I know I can't do as good a job as he could. But do you really think he could do his usual job feeling the way he does? With Skeeter not a hundred percent, we're all on equal footing here."

"And why should you be the one to lead?" the general asked. "Why not one of the other boys who will be going with you?"

"Are any of the others here volunteering?" Noah asked.

The general laughed. "No. No one seems to be beating down my door."

"Well then . . . ," Noah said.

The general hesitated, but finally he nodded. "All right, son. You're right, I guess, about Skeeter not being able to perform at his best. And you have been out there with him. You know the drill."

"You won't tell my uncle?" Noah asked, knowing that his uncle would convince the general to change his mind.

The general grimaced. "No. I won't tell him. But what about Skeeter?"

"Order the doctor to put him out," Noah said.

The general sighed. "All right. But I'll say one thing, Noah: If we do this, and we make it through, you'd better think about protecting me as much as you're protecting Skeeter."

"Protect you?" Noah asked.

"From your uncle," the general said. "'Cause he's going to be madder at me than a whole hive of hornets."

CHAPTER THIRTY-THREE

The evening of February 18 was dark and moonless. Quiet lay heavy on the town. Noah packed his rucksack with two days of cold rations, a canteen, a shovel for foxhole digging, ammunition, and first aid supplies.

He checked the nylon rope he would use for the climb, making sure it was free of flaws. He cleaned his rifle. His hands shook as he did this, and he prayed he would not have to use it.

Beside him Bill and Roger were packing their things, too. When he had finished, Noah slung his rucksack over his shoulder and picked up his gun. "I'm going to go on over and say good-bye to my uncle before he heads out for his final briefing."

Bill and Roger stood. Roger's enthusiasm for the climb had faded as the hour approached. He bounced from foot to foot, looking nervous. Outwardly, Bill still seemed calm, although Noah had seen him writing his girlfriend for two hours earlier that day.

"Good luck, Noah," Bill said. "I'll see you at the top."

Noah nodded and held out his hand. The boys shook their good-byes, saying nothing more. Noah opened the door of the cottage and slipped out into the night.

Above him, he could see Riva. The searchlights the Tenth Mountain Division had set up weeks earlier, which had been shining up at its peak every night since, were sweeping back and forth. They were intended to blind the enemy and give just enough light for the 86th to make their assault. The mountain had never looked as formidable as it did tonight.

The cottage where his uncle and the general were housed was dark. Noah found his uncle alone, sitting and staring at the wide, wooden floor. Noah slipped his rucksack off and squatted down in front of his uncle. "I just came to tell you good luck, Uncle Shelley."

James Shelley looked at Noah, and then reached out and pulled him into a hug, whispering, "You know how I feel about sentimentality and all that crap, so I'll just say this: Keep your head low, boy, and your wits sharp, and I'll see you in a few hours."

Noah laughed as he leaned back. "Don't go overboard, Shelley."

His uncle smiled for a minute and then stood. "Look, Noah, if anything should happen to me, Olaf and Skeeter promised to watch over you. I've got me a life insurance policy with your name on it. You take that money and go to college, do something for others with your life. It's what you were made for."

Noah stared up at his uncle in surprise.

"Aw" — James Shelley grinned, waving his hand in front of his face — "don't get too excited about the money. I ain't going to go that easily, you know."

He turned to leave.

"Be careful, Shelley," Noah choked out.

"You, too, boy," his uncle said.

His uncle swung up his rucksack and rifle and headed out the door. "You've grown into a fine man, Noah Garrett, a real fine man. I'm proud you're my nephew, you hear?"

Then he was gone.

Noah waited a minute or two, then slipped out and made his way to the hospital. He crept into Skeeter's room and found him sleeping soundly. He slipped on Skeeter's parka with Skeeter's insignia on it. He transferred his own equipment into Skeeter's rucksack with Skeeter's patches on it. He was just stepping out of Skeeter's room when he felt a hand on his shoulder. Noah jumped.

Sofia stood behind him.

"What are you doing here?" Noah asked in surprise.

"I came by truck this evening. I wanted to say *arrivederci* to all of you," she said. "I thought I'd see Skeeter first, and then I was coming to find you and your uncle. But what are you doing here? And why do you have on Skeeter's things?"

"Skeeter isn't strong enough to do this," Noah said. "Please don't tell my uncle."

Sofia gazed at him for a moment, and then slowly nodded. "I will pray for you, Noah."

Noah turned away, too choked up to respond. He bent and picked up his rifle from the floor. He swung it onto his shoulder and turned once more to look at Sofia. She smiled slightly.

Noah smiled back and then stepped out into the night. It was close to seven P.M., cold but not bitterly so. *This is it,* he thought. *We are attacking.* His heart beat hard against his chest. Noah took a deep breath. *But Skeeter,* Noah thought, *Skeeter will live.*

Once outside, he headed toward the hut that served as headquarters at the base of Riva Ridge. He went inside the darkened room, all the lights having been turned off to avoid any suspicion on the Germans' part. Noah stayed to one side, pulling Skeeter's hood close about his face. The other leaders of the various companies of the 86th were crowded into the room with them.

Daniel called out softly, "Skeeter's here now, General."

"Good," the general whispered. "Let's go over this one more time."

On the general's other side was Noah's uncle. He prayed his uncle would be too busy and the room too crowded for him to notice he wasn't Skeeter. Noah could feel sweat breaking out on his forehead.

The general's voice was soft and low in the darkness as he talked about the dangers and pitfalls and the strategies they would use on each path up the various sides of Riva Ridge. The constant warmth and refreezing had turned the mountainsides into walls of ice. The going would be difficult. Noah forced himself to concentrate on what the latest scouting party had reported back to the general.

James Shelley asked questions. Noah didn't dare ask any, but he grunted his understanding several times. It wasn't complicated. They had done the patrols often enough. He knew the mission. Climb and attack.

When the general finished, Noah moved away before his uncle had time to walk over and say any fond personal farewells. Instead, he nodded quickly, and James Shelley nodded back. For once, Noah was glad of his uncle's inability to talk about his feelings.

Noah stepped outside and gathered his group together by signaling with his hands and not speaking. Then he stood with them to one side, his eyes on the ground, while the general stood before them.

His eyes blurred over. *I'm going*, Noah thought. *I'm going to face the enemy tonight!* He felt himself begin to shake. Would he be alive at the end of the assault? Or would he lie on the ground halfway up Riva, snow covering his lifeless body? Images of Wiley filled his head. Noah snapped himself together sharply. He couldn't afford those thoughts now. If he was to have a chance at all, he had to concentrate.

"Men," the general spoke softly, "you go into battle tonight. It will not be easy. We can offer you no cover with planes, as that would give away the element of surprise, nor from tanks or jeeps, which can't maneuver the steep slopes. Some of you may die tonight. But I want you to know you die for a good cause, for God and for country."

Can you die for God? Noah wondered. He thought of all the battles in the Bible. *Yes*, he thought, *maybe you can*.

"I am proud," said the general, pacing back and forth, "proud of you all."

Then he turned and walked away, signaling the beginning of the climb up the mountain and the attack on Riva Ridge.

CHAPTER THIRTY-FOUR

Noah watched his uncle take his company off to climb up one side of the mountain. Other companies of the 86th moved off to their assigned spots circling the base of the ridge. Noah waved his hand, moving his own boys forward to the nearer side. The general came up to them, stopping them all for a minute. "Boys, I want you to know that tonight it's not Skeeter who will lead you. He was too sick to make it."

Noah pushed back his hood. The boys all stared.

"Jesus. Does Shelley know about this?" one boy whispered.

"No," the general replied curtly. "This is my decision. Noah is in charge. You will follow him."

One of the other boys swore under his breath.

Daniel stepped forward. "No more of that. I agreed with the general's decision. Skeeter was too sick to take on this climb. His weakness may have hindered our success. Noah may not be as experienced, but I, for one, believe he can do it. And I'm willing to put my life into his hands and trust his decisions. I expect the same from you, boys."

"You'll be covering from the rear?" someone asked.

"Yes," Daniel assured them.

Noah gave Daniel a grateful look. Daniel simply nodded and moved toward the back. Quietly, the boys fell into line, dividing into groups.

"Good luck, then, boys," the general said. He gave Noah one long last look, then turned and walked away.

Noah signaled to his company, and they began to walk single file up the trail that marked the beginning of their side of the mountain, each boy tapping the boy behind him when they were ready to move forward. Noah's heart beat hard against his chest.

It was easy going at first, but Noah knew the trail would soon give way to steep, sheer cliff sides. He and the boys walked slowly up the path, being careful not to dislodge stones that would warn the Germans they were coming. They spaced themselves far enough apart to prevent whipping tree branches from hitting one another in the face.

At the Dardagna River, the water raced icily by them. Noah stepped slowly across, planting each foot carefully on the logs that had been laid there for them. They were almost all across when one boy slipped and went in up to his waist in the freezing waters. The sound of the splash was loud in the quiet of the night. Everybody halted.

Noah scampered back over the logs to help the boy out, knowing as he did so that his movement would attract attention if there were Germans nearby.

"Do you need to go back?" Noah whispered, conscious of his voice, too. He shivered, imagining a German patrol popping up in front of them and the feel of a bullet in his chest.

The boy shook his head. "No, sir. I've got extra clothes."

"We'll wait while he changes, then," Daniel said, joining them. "No point in him getting frostbite."

Noah nodded, and they all stood to one side to let the boy change. Noah felt like screaming. He wanted to go, to get this thing over with before they were discovered.

At last, they were ready to move out again along the path. When they reached the end of the trail, Noah quickly unpacked his rucksack and began to set the spikes out ahead on the wall of the mountain. Softly, he tapped them in, passing the rope through that would keep his boys together on the climb.

When at last he was finished, Noah signaled to the boys behind him that they would start. He reached out and stepped up on the first toehold, then onto the second. Suddenly, the first hold gave way. Noah went tumbling backward.

The boys below reacted quickly. They caught him, breaking his fall.

"Are you all right, Noah?" someone whispered.

Noah nodded, though his heart was racing. That had been close. He hadn't considered dying in an accident before they even reached the top. He took a deep breath. He would have to be more careful.

He stood up and turned back to the cliff wall. "The rock is more brittle than the general anticipated," he said softly. "We'll have to use wedges and slits and the padded hammers."

They all nodded their understanding. Noah turned and rummaged in his rucksack for new footholds. The different equipment caused a dull *click* every time Noah hammered it into the rock. He could feel the hair rise on the back of his neck with each small sound. At last, they began to climb.

Sweat ran down Noah's face as they rose higher and higher toward the enemy. Each boy in the company carried almost one hundred rounds of ammunition on his back. They were walking explosives. Noah knew that they could easily be picked off by a German pilot or soldier — one good shot would blow them sky-high.

Slowly, they ascended. An hour passed. The wall of the mountain got colder and icier. Fog drifted in, making the going even more difficult. Noah rubbed his eyes, straining to see what lay ahead in the dark.

Farther away, he could hear the sound of the boys in the other groups climbing up. He reached out his hand to find the next spot for a toehold and felt nothing but ice. His fingers searched all around. The ice was rough and seemed to go on in a continuous pattern.

"What is it?" whispered the boy right behind him.

"We've come across a frozen waterfall," Noah whispered back.

"Can we get around it?" another voice softly floated up.

Noah felt around some more. It seemed to cover the whole

side of the hill, but there were parts where it wasn't too wide. "No. We'll have to cross it."

Cautiously, Noah felt his way across the slippery surface, searching for areas where the ice was thin or the width of the water was narrow. Slowly, the boys came along behind him, until at last, they were safely across.

Again, they began to climb. The sky began to lighten. Noah began to panic. It wouldn't be too long before they would be spotted.

He hammered in another foothold and then another. Then just before him, he saw that they had reached the summit. He signaled behind him that they were there. He didn't know whether to be relieved or terrified. He realized that when his head crested the top, he would be facing Germans. He swallowed hard. Slowly, he unhooked his rifle from his back and pulled himself upward.

A pair of boots and a gun came into view. Noah looked up to find a soldier standing above him.

CHAPTER THIRTY-FIVE

We beat you, Skeeter!" James Shelley crowed. "We beat you guys up here, and you now owe me one bottle of the best whiskey made in Italy!

"If they make whiskey here," he added. Then he stopped and stared. "Hey! What the . . ."

But Noah didn't hear the rest. He was looking at how many Germans his uncle's company had managed to capture and truss up like birds at a Thanksgiving dinner. Noah felt tears coming to his eyes, tears of thanks that he had not had to be involved but had still saved Skeeter the energy of the climb.

Then there was a hand on his jacket, and he was being yanked up.

"Watch it!" Noah cried out. "There are other men attached to the end of this rope!"

His uncle let go and set Noah down. His eyes bored into Noah's as the rest of Noah's company scrambled up to the summit.

Noah stood, looking at the ground. The boys moved away quickly, leaving Noah alone to face his uncle's anger.

"What," began James Shelley icily once everyone was safely at the top, "were you doing out in front?"

"Skeeter wouldn't have made it. The general okayed it," Noah said, still not meeting his uncle's eyes, looking at the Germans instead.

The Germans looked frightened. *What must they be thinking?* Noah wondered. His heart went out to them. They had to be scared. One of the younger ones was fidgeting, wiggling around uncomfortably.

"He what?" Noah's uncle exploded.

"We knew you wouldn't agree to it," Noah mumbled, "so we just didn't tell you."

"We don't have time to talk about this now," Shelley said, "but, boy, you are in hot water when we get down from here."

Noah saw that the young German's one hand was free. Someone had not tied his ropes tightly enough. Then Noah caught his breath as suddenly the boy was swinging a gun around, aiming it at James Shelley.

"No!" Noah screamed. "Stop!"

James Shelley ducked, and everyone began to run toward the Germans. But it was too late. In the fury and hatred that Noah saw reflected in the German boy's eyes, he realized he had no choice. Noah pulled his rifle to his shoulder, aimed, and fired. The boy fell over in a heap.

Bill, Roger, and the others reached the Germans and quickly began to check the rope on the other soldiers while Daniel bent over the German boy, ripping away his gun. "He's been shot through the shoulder," he told them.

"Wow, Shelley," Roger said, finally standing. "He almost *had* you."

Noah's uncle swayed back and forth, his face strangely white.

"You saved your uncle's life, Noah," Bill said.

Noah stared down at the rifle in his hand. He felt a welling in his stomach. His hands began to shake. He dropped the gun, fell to his knees, and was sick.

His uncle knelt down beside him and held his head. "Keep a sharp eye on those prisoners for a minute, boys."

"I had to," Noah mumbled in between heaving. "I had to. I couldn't let him shoot you."

"You did what you had to, Noah," his uncle agreed, "what any good soldier would have done, what you were ordered to do."

Noah threw up again and again. He threw up until his stomach felt torn apart. Then Noah sat back wearily and wiped his mouth on his sleeve. "Are you okay, Noah?" his uncle asked, and Noah could hear the worry in his voice. "Are you okay, boy?"

With jerky motions, Noah forced himself to stand. Then, bending over, he picked up his rucksack.

"What are you doing, Noah?" his uncle asked.

Noah didn't answer. He walked unsteadily over to the Germans. The enemy soldiers all looked at him with wide, frightened eyes. Noah bent over the boy he had shot. The boy tried to move away, but Noah clamped a hand on his good shoulder and held him there firmly. The boy cried out.

Noah closed his eyes for a moment, seeing again the

hatred that had filled this boy's eyes. Then he looked directly at the boy.

"Noah," his uncle called, his voice sounding panicked as he stood and began to walk toward Noah and the Germans, "there are rules about the treatment of prisoners. What are you doing?"

"Hey, Noah," Bill said, reaching out for him. "Hey, buddy, you don't want to hurt him now, you hear? It's over, Noah."

Again Noah didn't answer. Roughly, he pushed the boy's shirt to one side. The wound was deep.

"Nein! Nein!" the boy screamed out.

From his rucksack, Noah grabbed his first aid kit, pulling out bandages and iodine. Swiftly, Noah cleaned the wound and bandaged the shoulder. The slug was still in there, he knew, but at least he had stopped the bleeding.

When he was done, he raised his eyes to the German again. The young boy had grown still.

"You see?" Noah said to the boy. "We're not that different."

One of the other German soldiers spoke then, his words low and harsh. The wounded German boy turned to listen and then looked back at Noah. All the fury and hatred that Noah had seen there seemed to drain from him.

"Danke," he whispered.

"He says thank you," the other German soldier translated.

Noah nodded.

"Aw, what'd you go and save him for?" Roger complained.

Noah looked up at his friend. "Because I *had* to."

Slowly, Noah put everything back in his rucksack. His uncle helped him to his feet. In the distance, they could hear the sound of gunfire. The rest of the 86th regiment, coming up the other side of Riva, was obviously still battling it out for control of their portion of the ridge.

"That was a fine thing you did there, Noah," his uncle said.

Noah shrugged. He had seen heroic things and horrible things recently in equal measure. Perhaps he just meant to push the scales to one side, at least for a tiny slice of time.

"Boys," Shelley commanded, "let's round these men up and get them down the mountain."

He turned to Noah. "And when we get down from here, I'm going to insist the general assign you to hospital duty permanently. After tonight, he owes me. I've been thinking about this ever since that doctor pointed out how helpful you were there."

Noah just nodded. He was too weary to argue.

"I want you back in the hospital and out of this," his uncle continued. "I want you away from here."

Noah nodded again. He had saved Skeeter. He had saved his uncle and this German boy, but he couldn't save the world. Not by himself. Not at sixteen.

"I was thinking about being a doctor," Noah said, rubbing his eyes with the back of his hand. "We live through this, Shelley, I think that's what I'll do."

"Yeah?" his uncle said. "Then maybe some good will come out of this war after all, Noah boy."

Noah didn't answer. What could he really say? Maybe something good would come of it, but would any of them know until time had passed? War, Noah saw now, was the great gamble, sometimes necessary, sometimes not. Only time, sometimes years and years of it, could truly tell if it had been worth it. For no matter the outcome, there was always one sure bet: Many people would pay the price of it. Wiley, Cam, Sofia's father, Daniel's family — they had been war's victims. Today, it had almost been his uncle.

There was nothing to do now but pick up and go on, take a deep breath, draw up the strength from his upbringing in the flat farmland of his home, and face whatever lay ahead in the peaked and jagged mountains of the rest of his life.

"Come on, Noah," his uncle said. "Let's get these men to the camp below."

Noah nodded and followed James Shelley, helping the Germans to their feet. And together, the Germans and Americans began the long climb down Riva Ridge.

The Phantoms, or Tenth Mountain Division, were an actual skiing division that made the assault on Riva Ridge and Mount Belvedere in February 1945. By capturing these mountains, they turned the tide of the war in Italy. Many in the military considered their purpose frivolous, but in Italy, the Phantoms proved those skeptics wrong. The attack on Riva and Belvedere and the subsequent push into the Po Valley proved not only their incredible mountaineering skills, but also their courage and their willingness to give their lives for their country.

Many of the Phantoms, like Olaf, came from northern Europe: Finland, Norway, and Sweden. They were already great skiers and resistance fighters, and they helped train their American counterparts at Camp Hale.

Before they left for Europe, the Phantoms were known for their wild exploits in Colorado. Two Phantoms actually did challenge each other to the hike James Shelley made, seventy-five miles with only one candy bar for provisions. They also did radio to a pilot who was flying below them as they skied at a higher altitude. Once, just for fun, they scaled the sides of Leadville's Vendome Hotel, giving the guests a terrible fright. They escaped without getting caught.

The maneuvers on Ptarmigan Peak and the training for all recruits were real and as vigorous as described in this book. During World War II, kids could sign up as early as fifteen (although in this book, I made the age sixteen) with their parents' permission, and many did. Everyone was excited to go and "beat those Germans," but few understood the dangers and misery of battle.

Many were also unaware of the horrors of extermination that were occurring daily under the Nazi regime. Although the atrocities had been reported in newspapers as early as 1942, the articles were usually only a sentence or two, buried deep in the back pages of the paper. It wasn't until September 1944, when a picture of the shoes of the exterminated victims was printed, that most people in the United States became aware of what was actually happening in Europe. (In my story, I had the story appear earlier in the year to help aid Noah in his decision to go to Italy.)

After the war, many Phantoms found that they missed the excitement of being in the mountains. Skiing, as we know it today, was not a popular pastime in the United States yet. But because of the Phantoms and their love of the sport, there are now ski schools in New England, the Sierra Club, and two famous resorts in the Rockies: Aspen and Vail. All were started by Phantoms.

In Colorado today, there exists a backcountry trail system from Vail to Aspen. The trail was made in honor of the Tenth Mountain Division. Skiing enthusiasts can actually trace the footsteps of these brave soldiers by skiing their paths, staying in a series of huts that have been built along the trail.

This story came to me, as most of my stories do, in such a way that I could not ignore the call to write it. My husband first made me aware of the Tenth Mountain Division when he saw an article in *Sports Illustrated* about the cross-country skiing trail that had been created in their honor. Rather than being interested in *doing* the actual skiing, I was fascinated by the *story* of the skiing Phantoms. I began to do research. And I began to write the book.

The following summer, I was at a tennis match at my husband's summer cabin, which is on a mountain in the Berkshires. This place is very secluded, and on the lake, there are only seven camps. As I was talking that day to one of the camp owners, Peter Binzen, a man of many talents, I happened to mention the subject matter of my book. He turned to me and began to laugh. Peter Binzen was a Phantom! Not only had *he* built a camp on the lake, but there were *three others* on the lake as well, and I had not even known it!

Now these men are no longer Phantoms to me but actual flesh and blood, men who were true heroes during World War II. I am honored to have told a small part of their story.

REFERENCES

Casewit, Curtis W. *The Saga of the Mountain Soldiers: The Story of the 10th Mountain Division.* New York: Julian Messner, 1981.

Chamberlain, Tony. "Tenth Is Called." *Boston Globe*, February 25, 1999.

Dawidoff, Nicholas. "Atten-hut, You Skiers!" *Sports Illustrated*, December 18, 1989.

Jenkins, McKay. *The Last Ridge: The Epic Story of America's First Mountain Soldiers and the Assault on Hitler's Europe.* New York: Random House, 2003.

Johnson, Norma Tadlock. *Soldiers of the Mountain: The Story of the 10th Mountain Division of World War II.* Baltimore: PublishAmerica, 2005.

Shelton, Peter. *Climb to Conquer: The Untold Story of World War II's 10th Mountain Division Ski Troops.* New York: Scribner, 2003.

Tenth Mountain Trail Association Newsletter. Aspen, CO: Vol. 2, No. 4, December 1989.

Whitlock, Flint, and Bob Bishop. *Soldiers on Skis: A Pictorial Memoir of the 10th Mountain Division.* Boulder, CO: Paladin Press, 1992.

ACKNOWLEDGMENTS

In attacking the story of the Tenth Mountain Division, I had many compatriots who soldiered along beside me to produce this book.

To my agent, Bill Contardi: Thanks for your amazing scouting expedition for this manuscript. You led the charge and mapped the absolute best route for its publication. Here's hoping we have many more successful assaults together!

To my editor, Jody Corbett: You are the greatest of drill sergeants, whipping this manuscript into shape and ensuring that it was the best it could be before shipping it out. I am so thankful for your insight and your dedication to your craft.

To my copy editor, Lindsey Alexander: Thank you for ensuring that all my "equipment" was free of flaws. You wielded a strong pen with a light touch, and I am grateful to you for lending me your knowledge and skills.

To Shane Rebenschied, who created the cover art; Lillie Howard, who designed the cover; and Kristina Iulo, who designed the interiors: Thank you for rescuing Noah from the confines of my pages and giving life to him in such an intriguing and mysterious fashion. He truly looks a Phantom!

To the sales staff at Scholastic: It is your battle now, and I thank you in advance and from the bottom of my heart for all your hard work in helping *Phantoms in the Snow* to victory.

To Peter Binzen: Thank you for providing me cover as I headed out up the mountain, taking the time to read and check my facts as I told the Phantoms' story. I have always admired you so very, very much.

To my writing group, Anne Broyles, Donna McArdle, and Marcia Strykowski: Thanks for steadying me on those dangerous spots as I tried to balance my way along the slippery slopes of early drafts.

To my husband, Chris: For questioning my facts, correcting my grammar, and ignoring me when I was ready to settle for less than my best, I thank you for supporting me as I continue to struggle to make the climb toward writing excellence.

As always, to my daughters, Tobey and Liza: In the process of writing this book, I have seen you grow from girls to women. What a journey it has been. You are both the light of my life. May you always remember to be grateful to those who have given their lives to grant you the freedom to follow your dreams. I am so proud of you both.

And finally, to those men and women who serve this country, I am eternally grateful!

Kathleen Benner Duble is the acclaimed author of many children's novels, including *The Sacrifice*; *Bravo Zulu, Samantha!*; *Quest*; and *The Story of the Samson*, among others. She first heard of the Phantoms when her sports-crazed husband tried to convince her to ski the hut-and-trail system built on the soldiers' old training grounds. The trail covers 79 miles and rises over 11,500 feet into the mountains. Kathleen politely declined the invitation to sweat that much, but she did take up the challenge to write a small part of the Phantoms' story — discovering to her delight (after finishing the story) that she actually *knew* a few of these brave men!

Kathleen lives with her husband and their two daughters in Massachusetts. Visit her at her website: www.kathleenduble.com.